PERFECT BLUE

AWAKEN FROM A DREAM

PERFECT BLUE: AWAKEN FROM A DREAM

PERFECT BLUE –Yume nara samete
© Yoshikazu Takeuchi 2002

Originally published in Japan in 2002 by
SHUFU TO SEIKATSU SHA CO.,LTD., Tokyo.
English translation rights arranged with
SHUFU TO SEIKATSU SHA CO.,LTD.,Tokyo,
through TOHAN CORPORATION, Tokyo.

Seven Seas books may be purchased in bulk for promotional,
educational, or business use. Please contact your local
bookseller or the Macmillan Corporate and Premium Sales
Department at 1-800-221-7945, extension 5442, or by
e-mail at MacmillanSpecialMarkets@macmillan.com.

Follow Seven Seas Entertainment online at
sevenseasentertainment.com.

TRANSLATION: Nathan A. Collins
COVER ILLUSTRATION: Arvin Albo
COVER ART DIRECTION: Rafael Cal-Ortiz
COVER DESIGN: Nicky Lim
INTERIOR LAYOUT & DESIGN: Clay Gardner
PROOFREADER: Jade Gardner, Michelle Danner-Groves
ASSISTANT EDITOR: J.P. Sullivan
LIGHT NOVEL EDITOR: Jenn Grunigen
PRODUCTION ASSISTANT: CK Russell
PRODUCTION MANAGER: Lissa Pattillo
EDITOR-IN-CHIEF: Adam Arnold
PUBLISHER: Jason DeAngelis

ISBN: 978-1-626927-41-4
Printed in Canada
First Printing: April 2018
10 9 8 7 6 5 4 3 2 1

PERFECT BLUE

Awaken from a Dream

WRITTEN BY

Yoshikazu Takeuchi

TRANSLATED BY

Nathan A. Collins

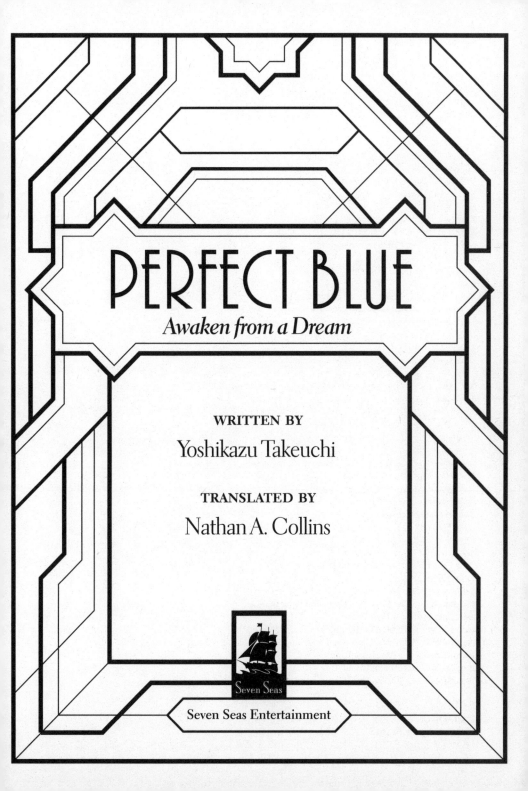

Seven Seas Entertainment

CONTENTS

1

WAKE ME
— FROM —
THIS DREAM

◇

A PULSING, NUMBING PAIN ran from the deepest folds of Toshihiko's brain into the tangled tendrils of his nervous system. On the back of his retinas, dull reds and blues pulsed and flashed, their faded hues like washed-out dollops of distempered paint. A strange sound filled his ears, like the grinding of unoiled gears.

Toshihiko awoke.

Fat beads of sweat clung to his forehead. They felt cold on his skin.

Sitting up on his thin, single-layer futon, he quickly shook his head a few times before taking in a deep breath.

He felt a pain in his chest.

Lowering his head, he pressed his fingers against the back of his neck and was met with a sharp jolt of displeasure.

He felt like he'd just had a bad dream. He couldn't remember what it was, but somehow, he was sure it hadn't been pleasant. He thought he remembered there being a woman with plastered-on makeup; her bright red lips had twisted into a crumpled smile as she let out a shrill squeal of a laugh.

His forehead was sticky with sweat. His heart was beating fast.

Beside his bed stood a table whose plywood veneer had begun flaking at the edges. On the table was a twelve-inch tube TV, left on. The screen glowed in monochrome static, the snow-like pattern punctuated by pulsing flashes in the signal, each flash accompanied by an abrasive noise like a cicada's call.

When did I fall asleep? Toshihiko wondered.

Irritated, he reached out to switch off the source of his nightmare (or at least, what he thought had been the likely source).

When he flicked the TV switch, the room went suddenly dark. He looked to his alarm clock. A little past six in the morning.

Pressing the thumb and forefinger of each hand against his throbbing temples, Toshihiko slowly got to his feet. He went over to his window and threw open the faded curtains.

Early morning sunlight filtered through the cracked, frosted window and filled his cramped four-and-a-half tatami mat room. But to the man newly awakened from a nightmare, even that gentle light felt sharp enough to slice into his flesh.

It stung his eyes.

As if chased away by the sun, Toshihiko retreated into the darker, malodorous kitchen. A pile of old dishes had amassed in the sink. Among them were rice bowls with dried-on grains, plastic spoons stained yellowish brown from instant curry, and glass cups half filled with cola long since gone flat.

Toshihiko pushed the dirty dishes to one side of the sink and turned on the tap. When the water gushed out, it smelled of chlorine. He cupped his hands and delivered a drink to his mouth.

Clouded with impurities, the water's unpleasant taste struck the back of his throat. With an equally unpleasant sound, Toshihiko spat the water back out.

He felt nauseous. Fighting the sensation, he took in another mouthful of water, then spat it out again, repeating the process two more times.

Beside the sink sat a small bar of soap, cracked and dried out, with spots of mold growing on its surface. Toshihiko picked up the soap and rubbed it back and forth between his hands. Hardly any bubbles formed, but he used it to wash his face anyway.

He let out a deep sigh.

He felt the slightest bit better now.

Next to the sink was a single gas burner—lonesome, rusted, cheap. Toshihiko filled a pockmarked aluminum kettle with tap water and placed it on the cooktop.

He pressed the gas burner's ignition switch. No flame appeared. Grease and dust had gummed up the auto-ignition mechanism, leaving Toshihiko no choice but to use a 100-yen lighter instead. He nearly burned his fingertips in the process, but at least he got the burner lit.

He reached into an adjacent cabinet with a fallen-off door and retrieved a jar of faintly moist instant coffee and a cup with a chipped rim and a panda on it. A crack ran right down the panda's face. He absentmindedly tapped his fingers on the cup's handle while he waited for the water to boil.

As Toshihiko stared at the kettle's spout, which contained a few extra bends beyond the ones it came with, he found himself suddenly overcome with sadness. Tears began to well in his eyes.

Next year, I'll be thirty, he thought. *I can't believe it.*

He felt keenly aware of the loneliness that came with solitary living. It crawled stickily up his back like a slime-coated slug.

Eight years had already passed since he dropped out of college.

Time has gone so fast.

If he had graduated like he was supposed to, found a

career like he was supposed to, he would probably have been promoted to section chief or some other managerial role by now. At the very least, society would have recognized him as a respectable, working adult.

He could have owned his own home, albeit a modest one, in which he could have lived happily with a wife and child.

When he pictured it all, a masochistic smile came to his face.

Toshihiko was lazy by birth. He was under no illusions—attempting to delude himself otherwise would have been far too much work. When he was still in college, he never went to his classes. Nor did he go out with any girls. He was the kind of person who avoided interacting with other people.

It wasn't that he lacked that common, human desire to go out and have drinks with friends, go on dates with women, and share in other such social experiences. If anything, he desired them even more than the typical person. But Toshihiko was excessively timid and shy to a fault. He found himself unable to approach members of the same sex, let alone women.

He was a pitiful man.

Not only was he timid and shy, he was unkempt, unclean, and indolent.

He wasn't simply lazy; he took laziness to the extreme.

Needless to say, he truly loathed having to work.

The entire history of his work experience could be summed up by day-wage part-time jobs taken up only by necessity whenever his funds ran dry—jobs he dropped as soon as possible. Consequently, his life was one of constant and extreme poverty.

Most of his meals came ready-made in packets. His biggest luxury was the one beef-and-rice bowl he allowed himself per month.

After all other expenses were accounted for, he had hardly any money left over to spend on clothing, and the clothes he wore showed it.

Had he some fashion sense, he might have been able to make it work, but he didn't, not even a shred. When he chose to loiter around the neighborhood outside his shabby apartment, it was in a sweat-stained T-shirt and outmoded bell-bottom jeans.

Take a moment to consider how cold the world would be to a man in his thirties, with no style, no money, no guts, no ambition, no friends, no hygiene, and a greater-than-average longing for the opposite sex.

To make matters worse, Toshihiko was short. His face was, as a matter of course, ugly. His hair, matted with grease and sprinkled with dandruff, was dreadful. His angular, bony features resembled the leftover parts of an amberjack fish, already gutted and filleted, and his eyebrows were off-putting and scraggly like dried kombu flakes. Below his bulbous nose rested slug-like lips that carried a vaguely oily sheen. Meanwhile, his eyes—somehow only his eyes—were round and pleasant, even innocent, in a way.

Each of these parts had been assembled into a countenance that was as clumsily put together as a face could be. If he were to work up the courage to approach anyone and offer them his diffident smile, that person—no matter how kind or compassionate—would likely turn tail and run.

Of that, Toshihiko was all too aware, painfully so.

The awareness shackled him, gradually drawing him ever deeper into the shell of his social phobia. He avoided social engagement, afraid he might offend anyone unfortunate enough to interact with him.

Toshihiko put a scoop of the instant coffee powder into his panda bear cup. Then he poured in the boiling water and swirled the contents. Wisps of steam ascended to his nose, but the stale coffee offered no aroma.

As he sipped the coffee, devoid of any flavor but bitterness, Toshihiko returned to his four-and-a-half tatami mat living space.

With the grunt of a man twice his age, he sat cross-legged on his futon mattress.

He let out a short sigh.

His mouth felt scratchy, but he didn't think the bad coffee was to blame. A stabbing pain throbbed in his head, and he felt nauseous. He hadn't felt right since he woke up. If anything, the nausea in his chest was gradually worsening, like some insect had eaten the upper half of his torso away.

Toshihiko shook his head vigorously a few times, then downed the rest of his coffee in a single gulp.

He coughed. Pain shot through his chest.

This was starting to get troubling. Toshihiko held his hand against his chest and thought, *I think I might be sick.*

A little over a dozen Betamax L-500 video cassette tapes stood in a row on Toshihiko's table.

These cassettes were his most prized treasure—his *only* treasure. By shaving away at his food budget and skipping a rent payment here and there, he had slowly but steadily built his collection.

He had purchased a tape deck for 9,000 yen from a used electronics store in the Nihonbashi district. With its recording head, he etched his only fantasies onto the magnetic tapes.

What he dreamed of were pop idol singers.

When real life refused to fulfill what he lacked, he directed his longings toward the illusory images painted by the scan lines of the cathode ray tube.

He checked idol singer magazines for upcoming TV appearances of his favorite performers and taped nearly every show.

Unlike real people in the flesh, once recorded, the idols would never betray him. Recordings could be watched whenever he wanted to, for as long he wanted to. The idols never looked at him with the contempt normal women did, as if they had seen something dirty and repulsive.

No, the idols always looked at him with a smile.

To Toshihiko, starved of both emotional and physical love, the idols' smiles seemed like those of angels.

He inserted a cassette into the tape deck and turned on the TV. He pressed the play button, and warm hues filled the screen.

Surrounded by colorful lights and a dazzlingly vibrant set, a slender young woman in a yellow dress kicked up legs so pale they might have been transparent. She sang passionately, a charming little song.

I love, love, love, that bashful you.
No matter how deep and strong my feelings
You pretend not to notice.

At the final chorus, the camera cut to a close up on the young singer's face. She brushed her left hand through her hair, silky and a little short, and curled her cherry blossom lips in a coquettish smile.

Her name was Asaka Ai. She had debuted with the song "Lemon Season" two years ago, and while she wasn't among the biggest names, she still maintained a respectable amount of popularity.

Though Toshihiko didn't quite understand why, she was his favorite idol. Perhaps her inability to make it to the top resonated with his own life.

But more than anything, Toshihiko admired how earnest she was. Ai was always kind and courteous to the TV show hosts and the other talent with whom she shared appearances, as well as to the behind-the-scenes staff—though the last part was just Toshihiko's guess.

He had watched his videotapes of her countless times. When a tape ended, he would rewind it and immediately watch it again from the beginning. For nearly every day in the past week, he'd done nothing but hole up in his small apartment watching his tapes of her again and again.

His feelings toward Ai surpassed the boundaries of a simple fan. He wanted to talk to her, if only just once. He wanted to go on a date with her, if only just once. Here he was, nearly a thirty-year-old man, believing these fantasies with total sincerity. It wasn't normal.

It was clearly abnormal.

He wanted to kiss her. He wanted to have his arms

around her. And yes, he wanted to have sex with her.

In the confines of his dingy apartment, his desires had escalated unchecked.

He thought about what he could do about it all.

He considered researching her schedule to find a time and a place where he could meet her in person. He wanted to talk to her, face-to-face, and pour out all his feelings. He wanted her to understand the passion he carried for her.

He wanted Ai to see him as a real person.

But there was a problem.

He didn't want Asaka Ai to see his ugly face—there was no way he could allow that. His atypical, even zombie-like features were not fit to be seen by her.

He wanted to meet her. He wanted it so badly he felt like he might die.

But he couldn't. With his face and the life he led, he could never meet her.

Nevertheless, his heart ached in yearning.

He hugged his arms around the TV, where Asaka Ai remained on the screen, and his inner voice cried out from deep within.

Ai... Ai-chan...

He squeezed his arms tight. The TV's plastic shell creaked under the pressure. Tears trickled down from Toshihiko's eyes.

He had rejected the world and its realities, and for that, his love for Ai had grown all the deeper, all the more severe. Over time, his thoughts had reached a terrible conclusion.

I will kill Ai, and myself.

It was no joke or simple passing thought. He was seriously considering acting on the idea.

His gaze went to the kitchen and to the sliding-door cabinet beneath the sink, where he kept his kitchen knife. It was brand new, purchased recently.

He looked again at Asaka Ai on his TV screen and then back to the cabinet.

His lips twisted into a smile.

.

For the past few days, Toshihiko hadn't set foot outside his apartment. He had eaten hardly anything. He was hungry but felt no desire to eat. Drinking only his bitter coffee, he sat in his gloomy room, watching his videos of Ai. He'd watched them from morning until night.

Both mentally and physically, Toshihiko was strained to his limits. He couldn't stop crying. He cried in loud, heaving sobs. Atop his flimsy futon—which he never bothered to fold and store away—and amid the hanging, raw stench of old sweat and dried semen, the nearly thirty-year-old man cried and wailed the name of a girl around half his age whom he'd never even met. He cried, and he cried, and he cried.

Thud.

The strange sound had come from his cracked, frosted window.

Toshihiko went over to it and threw open the curtains. In the span of a moment, a shape passed across the glass, and then it was gone. He thought it looked like a stooped-over person, but it might have just been a trick of his imagination.

Toshihiko became aware of a dull, lasting pain in the left side of his chest, just above his heart. He moved his hand up and pressed down where it hurt.

His flesh squished under his hand.

The shock registered not in his mind but as a physical, electric force that shot through his body. For a moment, his thoughts went blank. Then, hesitantly, he felt at his chest again.

His hand felt a small, plump softness.

His face went pale with stunned confusion.

He probed the protrusion with his fingers. As he squeezed at the softness, he wondered, *Am I sick?*

His grimy, flabby chest felt as if it had taken on the gentle firmness of a woman's breast.

He opened the top of his pajama shirt to look inside, and there it was. A breast. Two of them, even. He'd never seen a woman's breasts in real life before.

Two tiny, pink points stood in areolas wrinkled by emotional distress. His stale, sweaty odor had been replaced with a fresh, feminine scent not unlike a baby's milky smell. His skin wasn't the familiar oily yet dried out and cracked mess he was used to seeing, but was instead smooth, like moistened porcelain.

Toshihiko couldn't believe it was real. He thought he might still be caught in that earlier nightmare. The deep, throbbing pain persisted in his head.

That's what this is, he thought, taking great efforts to convince himself. *This is a nightmare.*

His mental state had been pushed too far to accept it as real. He was far too fragile for such a leap.

But reality was not to be denied as some dream. He had no choice but to accept the truth because it wasn't just his chest.

Appearing from the sleeves of his pajamas were a set of arms, and hands and fingers and palms, that were not as they had once been. His smooth skin was so pale it might have been transparent.

He put his hands in his hair to see if it too had changed. What he found wasn't his familiar mane, held stiff not by styling gel, but by accumulated oils. No—the hair he found was healthy, smooth, and flowing.

He touched his face. Gone was his angular, bony structure. In its place were petite features, from his eyes, to his nose, his mouth, and his lips, which were as soft and supple as freshly picked cherries.

Toshihiko ran to the kitchen. Somewhere on the windowsill above the sink, he had left a mirror. Impatiently, he picked it up. Its reflective mercury backing had begun to chip away.

He looked at his face and his heart nearly leaped out of his mouth. He gulped reflexively.

The face looking back at him had skin as pale as if it were dusted with flour. Its cheeks had a faint, healthy red tinge to them. Its eyes were bright and black. Its nose was dainty, and its lips were moistened. It was the face of an angel.

It was the face of his beloved Asaka Ai.

The resulting shock was tremendous. Toshihiko retained his thoughts and his personality, but his body had transformed—into the idol Asaka Ai.

Unable to cope with the shock, he let out a crazed scream that resounded through the apartment, otherwise quiet in the early morning.

The voice, too, was as pretty and clear as a ringing bell.

An hour had passed.

Toshihiko had finally calmed himself. He sat up on his futon and began turning an analytical eye toward the situation he now faced.

From the top of his head to the tips of his toes, he had completely transformed into Asaka Ai. But whatever had happened to his body on the outside, his insides all seemed to be in working order. In fact, he felt better now than he had as Toshihiko.

What luck, he thought. *What luck that I don't have any friends. What luck that I don't socialize. My parents— my only family—never leave the countryside. That means that I get to live the rest of my life here in this apartment with Asaka Ai.*

As soon as he came to that realization, shivers of delight ran through his body.

Because he had little in the way of friends or acquaintances, hardly anyone ever came to visit his apartment. He would be able to stay there with her forever, with no one to interfere. His most beloved idol was his, and his alone, to do with as he pleased.

Until this moment, he had wished someone would wake him from this dream. Now he wished that, if it was indeed a dream, no one would ever come to disturb him from it.

In body, he was Asaka Ai, but in mind, he remained himself.

Before long, he realized that he could play with her body however he wished.

He only had one fear.

What if Ai-chan (that is, he himself) were found by someone? He might be accosted by some strange man.

He thought back to the suspicious figure he'd seen in the frosted glass window but shook his head vigorously to cast away his worry.

He wanted Ai-chan to remain his forever.

For now, Toshihiko thought in an attempt to reassure himself, *I just won't leave the apartment.*

Now was not the time to worry. It was the time to thank the heavens for bestowing him with such an opportunity—and to enjoy it as much as he possibly could.

Slowly, Toshihiko began removing his pajama shirt. The dirty fabric slid away to reveal naked skin that practically shined in comparison. His shoulders carried a gentle, seductive slope, and on his chest were two pert breasts.

Toshihiko ogled his naked form with all the greasy lust of his almost thirty-year-old male mind.

Captivated by the beauty of his breasts, he cupped one in each hand and lifted them from below. He pinched his nipples between his thumbs and forefingers and felt the rush of a deep thrill only women could understand.

With the perverse stare of a man, Toshihiko watched as the idol groped her own chest. He experienced the act from both sides at once, the woman's physical pleasure and the man's emotional thrill. He squeezed Ai's breasts so hard the sensation edged into pain, and he let out a wordless moan.

Driven by his ecstasy, he removed his pajama pants. Thrusting out from his yellowed briefs were the two athletic legs he had so thirstily watched on his television screen.

Toshihiko traced his fingers up from his calf to the top of his thighs. When his hand reached his briefs, he yanked them off without pause. Toshihiko's inner thoughts revealed themselves on Ai's sweet face, twisting the charmingly cute features into ugliness.

Toshihiko's eyes fixated on a single point. With full intensity, his male gaze bore down upon the meeting point between Ai's pale thighs. Toshihiko picked up the small mirror from beside him and drew it near the space between his legs.

In whispered awe, he said, "This... this is Ai's..." but the rest got caught in his throat.

His fingers wriggling like spider legs, he fondled her hidden place with unbridled lust.

Several hours later, his passion had ebbed. His body weary, Toshihiko lay on his futon.

On the TV near his bed, Asaka Ai was performing her newest song, while he watched in the form of the fully naked Ai. A perverse pleasure ruled Toshihiko's body.

As if in sudden recollection, Toshihiko snapped his fingers. With a grin, he stood up and went over to his cheap, freestanding canvas wardrobe. He opened the zippered front and withdrew a paper bag from the back.

Inside the bag was an eye-piercingly yellow mini dress with plenty of frills, a copy of one Asaka Ai frequently wore. He had bought it in secret, driven by his deep yearning for her.

When Toshihiko was alone, in the middle of the night, he had sometimes dressed himself as her. He had pretended to be her, then anguished over his unrequited love.

But now he really had become her.

His passions stirred at the thought of being able to embrace the real Asaka Ai, in her real dress. Fresh waves of emotion coursed through him.

Wearing the dress now, he spun in place. Its hem floated and danced in the air, exposing—for a brief moment—the naked form beneath.

It's beautiful, Toshihiko thought. Feverish shivers of delight ran through his body. He hugged himself, his arms crossing over his chest, and a new fountain of desire flooded through him.

Ai, Ai, Ai-chan, he cried out inside himself as he lay back down on the futon.

Suddenly, a feeling of dread came over him.

His eyes went to the window.

He could sense an unseen watcher's intense gaze upon him.

Toshihiko approached the window and looked through a small gap between the panes of frosted glass.

It was now evening. On the street, he caught glimpses of salarymen hurrying home and housewives shopping, but he saw no sign of the figure that had frightened him.

It must have been my imagination getting carried away, Toshihiko thought. He turned from the window and started toward the middle of the room.

That's when it happened.

At the corner of his vision, he thought he sensed something that didn't feel right. He put his eye up to the window.

A tall electric pole stood beside a house across the street. There, lurking in its shadow, was a stooped-over man trying to escape notice.

An indescribable terror gripped Toshihiko.

Toshihiko knew the man hiding behind the utility pole would come back to peek through the window into his room. The man was like Toshihiko had once been—timid and afraid of strangers but filled with incredible lust.

The thought made the soft, downy hairs of his body stand up on end.

He must be another sick fan like me, Toshihiko thought with certainty. And not just a fan of any idol singer—a fan of Asaka Ai. *He's been watching me— watching Asaka Ai—through the gap in my window.*

Toshihiko's right eyelid twitched. *He won't be able to contain his desire. He'll come back to watch again.*

Or, he thought as the blood drained from his face, *he might already be coming.*

Quickly, Toshihiko checked to make sure his door was locked. It was.

He let out a deep sigh of relief and collapsed onto his futon. Deep down, he wished that he was worrying over nothing, that he had nothing to fear. But he knew better. All he had to do was look inside himself to know exactly what that kind of person was thinking.

That kind of man was clever, if nothing else. He appeared meek but was capable enough of taking action.

And so, Toshihiko knew the man was coming.

He turned off the TV and made himself alert. He couldn't know from where the man would come. He couldn't allow himself to relax. He needed to watch, listen, and be ready.

Toshihiko heard strange footsteps in the hallway outside his apartment. They seemed to drag miserably across the floor.

It was him. Toshihiko knew it was him. The footsteps were not the product of an overactive imagination.

There, listen. Just as Toshihiko had dreaded, they stopped outside his door.

Knock, knock...knock.

Even the way he knocked was hesitant.

Hearing such a cowardly knock reminded Toshihiko of his former self, and the likeness sparked an angry irritation. The only thing to do to a man like that was to meet him head-on and tell him off.

Toshihiko approached the door and spoke. "Who is it?!"

It came out harsher than he'd intended. He felt as if he could see the man's stunned reaction on the other side of the door.

The man didn't respond. Toshihiko could hear him breathing heavily through his nostrils.

Toshihiko pressed his attack. "Who is it? What do you want?"

Still no response. The breathing became louder.

Toshihiko raised his voice. "If you don't have a purpose here, then leave. I'm calling the police."

Before he'd finished speaking, the footsteps ran off.

The cowardly man had withered and fled from Toshihiko's (Ai's) threats.

It was a relief. Exhausted from the fear and anxiety, Toshihiko slumped weakly to the floor in his entryway. There, he began to think.

He pictured his terrifying stalker fleeing red-faced, and he tried to imagine what that man was feeling.

What if that had been him—the man he used to be? If his beloved Asaka Ai had spoken to him like that, what would he have done?

Toshihiko considered it carefully.

First, he would have run away. He would have run, crying, as fast as he could.

But then what?

Filled with determination, the timid man had come to visit the idol in a once-in-a-lifetime act of courage. But he'd been flatly and coldly told off—and not just by anyone, but by his beloved idol. He wouldn't have the courage to come calling a second time.

The man was surely in emotional shambles now. He would never see Asaka Ai again.

If that had happened to Toshihiko, what would he have done?

He knew the answer without having to think about it.

There was only one answer.

I would kill Ai, and myself.

The terrible phrase, almost forgotten, filled his chest.

Toshihiko felt as if every pore on his skin closed up.

The man would have no other options available to him. He would watch Ai for the right opportunity, and he would act.

Slowly, quietly, the greasy man would come, knife in hand, with dreadful intentions.

Toshihiko closed his eyes and tried to shake the mental image. But no matter how hard he tried to banish it, the vision remained seared into his mind.

Resolving to protect Asaka Ai, and by extension himself, he stood and walked to the kitchen where he kept the thirty-centimeter-long kitchen knife he'd purchased to kill Ai, and himself. As he opened the cabinet under the sink, he grinned cynically at the strange irony that he would protect Ai with the very same blade he'd bought to kill her.

Toshihiko's heart froze. Cold sweat materialized on his forehead.

The knife was gone.

It had been there, but now it was gone without a trace.

Toshihiko put his hands to his head. Someone had stolen his knife. And he knew who it was. *That man.* Who else could have done it?

Skriiiiiikkk, came a noise.

Toshihiko jumped.

The sound had come from his window. Something sharp was scratching at the frosted glass.

Toshihiko hurried back to his room and looked to the window.

The tip of a blade was slowly scraping from left to right.

It's him, it's him. He's here. He's come with the knife to kill Ai—and me!

Toshihiko's body froze as if bound hand and foot. He couldn't even scream. His eyes were locked on the window.

Following the knife's path, a mop-like mass smushed and smeared against the glass. Toshihiko knew what it was—hair. The man was pressing his greasy hair against the window. Slowly, the knife and the hair moved right to left. The knife etched a thin, sharp gouge, and the oily hair left a wide slug's trail.

Finally, the knife and the hair reached the window's edge and disappeared.

Toshihiko wondered where the man had gone but quickly realized where—the man was going around to the apartment building's entrance.

His fear was not groundless. As proof, only moments later, those miserable, dragging footsteps returned to the hallway, before stopping right in front of Toshihiko's door.

Bang bang, came the knock. *Bang bang.*

Even upon hearing that ominous sound, Toshihiko remained frozen, standing in the middle of the room. He was too afraid to move.

The knocking became louder. *Bang bang!*

The man outside was timid no more. He had come in unwavering conviction. He would kill Asaka Ai.

Toshihiko needed to do something. The locked door provided no true safety. The man would break it down to come in, if that was what it took.

Toshihiko knew this. And yet, he couldn't move.

The knife sank into the thin, flimsy wood of the door. The blade's tip glistened as it jutted from the interior side. The man twisted the knife, widening the tiny slit it had made.

A thin finger reached in through the door. A jagged splinter cut into its flesh. Blood began to form along the scrape.

Undeterred by the injury, the man began prying at the board with nothing but his finger. More of his skin tore, and blood began dripping from his fingertip. Nevertheless, he kept pulling at the board.

Soon, he had created enough of an opening to slide his arm in and undo the latch. The door creaked quietly open, and the man stepped in, bathed in the red light of the sunset outside Toshihiko's window.

The man wore a sweat-stained T-shirt and dirty jeans. His greasy, matted locks clung to his angular face and curled into points on either side of his head. Catching the sunset's light, the two points shone like Astro Boy's hair. The man's hand gripped the sharp knife tightly.

Toshihiko saw that the knife was the same one he had bought.

The man took one step toward Toshihiko and then another.

Toshihiko knew he was about to be stabbed. He knew he had to run. But his body wouldn't move. The more he panicked, the more firmly frozen he became.

The man spoke.

"A-Ai-san! I... I..."

His voice sounded as if it came up from the depths of hell. The voice was clammy and unpleasant, like that of a drunk and frustrated salaryman shouting unintelligibly at a karaoke bar.

"Forgive me, Ai-san," the intruder muttered as he bowed his head repeatedly. "This was my only option."

Then, with an inhuman wail, he rushed toward Toshihiko with intense speed.

Toshihiko could see it in the man's eyes—

I will kill you, and me.

The stench of the man's body assaulted Toshihiko's nose. In the next instant, he felt a burning pain in his side, as if he'd been struck by hot tongs.

Blood began soaking through his yellow dress.

The man withdrew the knife. White fatty tissue clung to the blade, then spilled out and dangled from the open wound.

Toshihiko looked down at the yellow dress, the red blood, the white fat. He found a strange beauty in the colors.

The man took the bloodied knife in a reverse grip. He plunged it into Toshihiko's chest. The pain felt like a strip of tape pressed against his skin and then forcefully yanked off.

Unable to move, Toshihiko was at the mercy of the man's knife.

The wound went deep into his chest. Blood sprayed out in a fountain. In an instant, his yellow dress was yellow no more.

The man twisted the knife inside his chest.

A numbness spread from the wound. Toshihiko began to cough; blood burbled from his mouth.

As the man showered in Toshihiko's blood, he said, "Ai-san, Ai... You're beautiful. You're so cute." His voice rose into a crazed shriek. "You're beautiful. You really are. Every day, I've touched myself watching you. I've done it more times than I could count. You understand how I feel about you, don't you?"

The man's flushed face was right in front of Toshihiko's.

The man's features, angular and bony, resembled the leftover parts of an amberjack fish, already gutted and filleted. His eyebrows were off-putting and scraggly like dried kombu flakes. His nose was bulbous. His lips were slug-like, with a vaguely oily sheen, and his eyes were round and pleasant.

On the verge of unconsciousness, Toshihiko thought in sudden realization, *So, that's who he is.*

He understood.

The man had Toshihiko's face.

He had Toshihiko's smell.

He had Toshihiko's personality.

So, that's who he is.

He's... he's me.

The man looked into Toshihiko's eyes, then blinked in sorrow. Toshihiko felt an indescribable love for the man.

I'm going to die soon.

In those last moments, Toshihiko looked the man in the eyes with as much affection as he could and gave him a smile.

The man smiled back at him.

Still smiling, the intruder slashed his own throat open with the knife.

As he coughed, fresh blood spilled from his mouth. He tried to say something through the coughs but couldn't form the words.

To Toshihiko, it sounded like he had said, "Thank you."

The man was telling him, *Thank you for understanding how I feel.*

The two shared a blood-soaked embrace. They held each other tight for as long as their strength held out. Then, still entwined, they fell to the floor.

The two became one.

The sunset painted the room in deep, deep red.
It was a terribly tragic sight.
Why did it have to be so tragic?

2

CRY YOUR TEARS

◇

O N AN ORDINARY WOODEN DESK sat a picture of
a cute young woman, dressed in a yellow beret
and pleated yellow culottes. She posed flirtatiously in
the picture, not a personal snapshot, but rather a collectable photo for her fans.

Every bit as commonplace as the desk at which he
sat, a man stared at the photograph. His expression was
deeply intense, to the point of ghoulishness.

Soon, the veins at his temples began to visibly throb.
The large box cutter knife in his hand trembled in syn-
chronized pulses. He ran the fingers of his other hand
through his bristly, hedgehog-like hair and rustled it
about. His face was broad and pudgy; his small, cowardly
eyes seemed out of scale in comparison.

Now those eyes flashed with anger.

He raised the box cutter high. In the next instant, its tip
sliced through the air and embedded in the photograph

with a metal blade's characteristic twang.

Though no one was there to hear him, he whispered, "This time—and I mean just this time..." He trailed off, as the anger in his eyes built to a boiling rage, then said, "I'll forgive you. But never again."

He pulled the box cutter free and touched his pointer finger to its edge. He pushed the blade into his flesh. Flecks of blood sprayed out from the wound, speckling the woman's picture.

Despite the pain, the man gave an enigmatic smile. He looked back and forth between his sliced finger and the girl moistened with his blood.

Was it the forced smile of someone sad, holding back their tears? Was it one of frustration, of anger? Or was he happy?

No one but him could understand what emotions lay behind that smile.

With his bloodied hand, he reached for a small envelope at the edge of his desk. The paper was decorated with the kind of cutesy designs that would be right at home atop one of the desks at an all-girls' school. On the reverse side was a hand-drawn heart.

Suddenly, the man's expression turned grave, and he crushed the envelope in his hand. His eyes were those of a man in prayer.

Perhaps without knowing it, he repeated, "Never again."

Kawasaki Yuma entered the studio dressed in a geeky *Minky Momo vs. Godzilla* T-shirt and faded denim jeans.

A slightly aged hair stylist greeted her with a high-pitched "Good morning, Yuma-chan!"

Yuma returned the woman's greeting with a smile. "Morning!"

"He's here already," the stylist said. She patted the top of her head and showed a teasing grin.

Yuma dropped her voice. "You mean baldy? He beat me here?" Her prematurely bald manager's perpetually grinning face popped into her mind.

The stylist nodded. "Bando-san is in high spirits today."

"Really?" Yuma said. "Is it really that surprising that I got a commercial gig?"

"It's the first he's had since he started working with you. I don't think he could help being excited about it."

"I guess you're right."

Yuma gave the stylist a quick wave and went to the green room at the rear of the studio.

Bando, Yuma's prematurely bald manager, approached her. "Good morning, Yuma." He beamed so broadly that the smile brought creases to his face. "You look as adorable as ever. First-class idol singers like you are in a whole different league."

Yuma thought, *Always with the over-the-top flattery.* She found his silver-rimmed eyeglasses and sweaty forehead depressing. *And his hair is getting even thinner, too.* Her eyes landed on Bando's scraggly beard, and she smiled back at him uncomfortably.

"Yuma," he said, "this could be your big break. A commercial. A TV commercial!" Bando spoke so fast little bits of spittle flew. "Sure, it's only going to play in Tokyo, but this is Sanshin Denki. They're planning a huge promotional push with you representing their new line of electronics."

Inserting coins into a vending machine, Yuma muttered with disinterest. "I'm just there to get eyes on the ads of some local retail chain. We don't need to get so worked up over it."

"Yuma-chan, don't be like that. This is a commercial. A commercial! It's a lucky thing the company's president is a fan of yours."

Yuma took a gulp of her soda and shouted, "I hate that bald creep!" She made sure to put an emphasis on *bald*.

With a hint of a scowl, the stylist said, "President of a company or not, the guy's tastes *are* a bit creepy."

"Right?" Yuma said. "You think so, too—don't you, Makki?" She waved a pink costume in her hand. "Look at this awful thing. It's basically a cheerleader's outfit."

The stylist, Makki, said, "Wait until you see the hair style." She offered a photo for Yuma to see.

The photo was of a cute girl with pigtails.

"Seriously?" Yuma groaned. "That hairstyle, with this costume—that bald president is a total perv."

"Whatever the case," Makki said, as she braided the idol's shoulder-length hair, "his tastes are certainly…less than decent."

Yuma was seated in front of a full-length mirror. She watched as Makki's experienced hands transformed her hairstyle in no time at all. Looking at her new pigtails, Yuma had to admit she did look cute.

Makki said, "Yuma, you're adorable. With that pink mini on, you'll drive that old man wild."

"I just can't believe I turned eighteen, and now *this* is the costume I have to wear."

"Well, think of it this way. Not many grown women who want to dress that way could make it work even if they got the chance to try."

"That's a good point," Yuma said, as she stepped behind the curtain that separated the small dressing space from the hair and makeup room.

Alone behind the partition, Yuma smoothly discarded her T-shirt and jeans. Wearing only her underwire bra and bikini panties, she appraised herself in the mirror with a smile.

Her body had good proportions. Aside from her breasts, which were a little on the small side, her body curved in and out where it was supposed to. She put her hands on the sides of her waist. There was more give than she would have liked. It wouldn't do for modeling.

Darn it, she thought. *That's my only flaw.*

She remembered her boyfriend Yukio saying, "You're not getting enough exercise, are you? You're starting to get some fat on you."

She hadn't seen him for a little while now. Between rehearsing her new song and a string of nationwide promotional events, she hadn't the time to get together with him. Not long ago, in her hotel room, she watched his supporting-role performance in a TV drama and realized how much she missed him.

I think I might be falling in love, she had thought.

Still dressed only in her underwear, she smiled bashfully at the memory. Then, reining in her distracted thoughts, she said, "All right!" before quickly putting on her pink mini dress and stepping out of the dressing room.

Yuma twirled, sending the hemline of the pleated dress precariously high up her thigh.

Thoroughly impressed, Makki said, "You look super cute!"

With the nervous eyes of an herbivore, the man readied his finger on the VCR's record button. On the TV screen, three male pop idols performed an energetic choreographed dance. According to the program guide, *she* would be on next.

The trio's song appeared to be reaching its conclusion. The music swelled, and the three struck their final poses.

The man pushed the button.

There were a few seconds of silence, then a young woman appeared on the screen.

She wore a cowboy hat, wild bangs peeking down to touch the tops of her eyebrows. Her wide eyes shone, dreamlike. A cowhide vest covered her white blouse, and jean shorts accentuated her rowdy charm.

A star-shaped brooch, placed near her shoulder, served as her only adornment. Though simple, there was something inexplicably flirty about it.

The woman kicked up a slender leg that stretched all the way down from her high-cut shorts. Then she threw her microphone toward the camera.

She pulled back the mic's cord with her left hand, causing it to twirl in the air before returning to her grasp.

The move had been specially choreographed for this, Kawasaki Yuma's new song, "Lariat of Love."

As he watched her perform, the herbivore-eyed man grinned sloppily and bobbed his head up and down in time with the beat.

Under his breath, he said, "Yuma is putting everything into this song."

His face said that he knew all there was to know about Kawasaki Yuma. On the bookshelves behind him stood tightly packed rows of recorded videotapes. The spines were labeled with dry-transfer letters that read Idols I, Idols II, and so on, but most bore the same name: Kawasaki Yuma.

The wall beside the bookcase was covered floor-to-ceiling with overlapping posters. Most of those featured Kawasaki Yuma, too.

On the TV, Yuma finished the song's second chorus and moved on to the big finish.

I'll snare you with my burning love.
Oh, my lariat of love.

As she said the last word—love—Yuma again performed her microphone lasso trick. After the mic had finished tracing its arc through the air and she'd caught it firmly in her grasp, she held it like a pistol, then gave a wink and shouted, "Bang!"

And the song was over.

The man stopped the recording and hurriedly turned on his radio because *Yuma's Happy Talk* was to start at ten.

As he listened to the radio, he reviewed Yuma's schedule for the day in his head.

Her radio show was pre-recorded today, which means her live performance on Golden Music *was her last job for the day. After that, she's free. Tomorrow, she has a live appearance on another radio show at eight in the morning, which means she should be going straight back to her home tonight.*

The man imagined her out chatting happily with some guy instead of going home on her own. The thought of her with a man, even imagined, filled him with pain, followed by incredible rage.

She isn't seeing anyone, he told himself. *She couldn't be. Look at her charming face. A girl that innocent, that adorable, couldn't be seeing anyone.*

Big, fat tears dripped from his diminutive eyes.

I love her too much for that. I devote all my time to loving her. She wouldn't betray me with another man. Other women would, but not Yuma.

The man picked up a photograph from his desk. It was the collectable photo of Yuma from her early days.

He gazed into the grinning face of the yellow-bereted teen. He sighed and whispered words that came from the bottom of his heart. "Yuma, tell me the truth. There isn't any other man. There's only me."

Yuma didn't reply. She simply kept on smiling brightly back at him.

The man hugged the photograph to his chest. Then,

slowly, he raised it up to his face.

"Yu-Yuma…"

He pursed his ugly lips into something uglier and gave Yuma's face a wet, sloppy kiss.

In the small green room of a TV station, Yuma summoned tears to her eyes. She protested, "I'll always be a second-class idol—just a nobody in a miniskirt. That's why I've had to take every job that comes in. No one listens to my songs. They all just stare at my legs. Don't think I don't see that."

Flustered by her outburst, the balding Bando said, "Y-Yuma-chan, don't sell yourself short like that." He put his arm around her shoulder as he attempted to comfort her. "You're a terrific idol and a terrific entertainer!"

Yuma brushed away his arm. "If you actually think that, you should listen to what I'm saying. Do I really have to meet the president of that company in person?"

"Yuma-chan," the manager said. "This is your job. Sanshin Denki is putting their full weight behind promoting you. Surely you can at least meet the president and say a few words."

Yuma furrowed her eyebrows sharply. Filling her voice with acid, she said, "As long as that's all I end up having to do for him…"

"Don't be silly. Of course that's all. You don't have

to worry about a thing. But I want to be clear—I'm not asking you to do this. I'm telling you, as your manager, that I expect you to do it."

Yuma shook her head with a "Hmph," then threw open the green room door. "And let me guess—I'm supposed to put my hair in pigtails and wear that pink mini dress. Fine. But I'll tell you this: I'll meet him, we can have a little talk—but that's it."

The man's eyes were those of an elephant—an elephant, hesitant and motionless.

The man with elephant eyes stood frozen in place as he stared at a poster of Kawasaki Yuma hung up inside the train station. The poster was a B1-sized advertisement for Sanshin Denki, which everyone knew was nothing more than a sketchy retailer hawking electronics of questionable manufacture.

On the poster, Yuma's wind-tossed miniskirt had lifted to reveal her slim, athletic legs in near entirety. The posters hadn't been up very long, but they had already become extremely popular among the serious idol fans.

The cutesy pigtail look was a 180-degree change from her previous image, but apparently those other fans liked it.

In the poster, Yuma looked more girl than woman. The man stared into her face, his gaze intense enough to bore a hole through the paper.

"This is wrong," he muttered under his breath. "It's all wrong. This isn't Yuma."

Rage filled his elephant eyes as he withdrew the box cutter he'd concealed in his pocket.

He carved an X across Yuma's face.

Kawasaki Yuma stepped out of her taxi and immediately felt anxious. A strange tightness gripped her chest.

For a moment, she stood in front of her apartment building and took deep breaths to steady her nerves.

It was eleven at night. At this hour, the upper-end residential street was empty, with not even a stray cat in sight. She told herself that the solitude was the source of her disquiet, and continued into the apartment's entrance, where she entered her passcode on the security panel.

The door automatically slid open.

The building's security system provided safety, but Yuma always thought it felt impersonal, lacking in human warmth. Tonight, it made her feel relieved. She rode the elevator up to the fifth floor and walked down the short open-air hallway to her door, which she unlocked with a key. Each floor of the building only had two units, and Yuma was the only one who lived on the fifth floor. She had complete privacy here.

As she was about to enter her apartment, she heard something fluttering above her head. She turned toward the sound and saw an object wedged in the crack at the top of the door. She reached up and took it.

It was a letter-sized envelope.

Yuma tilted her head in confusion. *Who could have come and left this here?*

A stranger shouldn't have been able to get into the building. *Had it been left there by another resident?* She never really associated with any of her neighbors…

Was it Yukio? she thought, picturing his tanned face. *But he has his own key. If he were here, he would have gone inside.*

Who, then, could it be?

Yuma's anxious worry returned. She flipped the envelope over.

Written in the rounded, distinctive characters that typified girlish handwriting were the words, *From Someone You Know.*

She had no idea who that could be. But something about the envelope tugged at her attention.

The rounded handwriting was cutesy, but somehow ominous. It presented an uneasy mismatch with the words it formed—adolescent characters making a formal announcement, *From Someone You Know.*

If words and handwriting could reveal a person's character, what kind of person would have written this?

Yuma felt an indefinable worry. Someone had slipped

through a hole in the building's security system to come to her home; that much was certain. That person then put a letter into the crack of her door.

With trembling fingers, she tore open the envelope to find out what was inside.

The smell of sweet perfume met her nose. Inside the envelope, she found a single page of scented stationery. She unfolded it and read.

> *I'm not mad at you.*
> *I'm not mad at you, because I believe in you.*
> *I'll even forgive your thoughtless actions—*
> *I understand that poster was part of your job and*
> *that you didn't have any choice but to do it.*
> *But that look wasn't you. No, no, it wasn't.*
> *I might even start to not like you anymore…*
> *That was a lie. Just a lie!*
> *I could never hate you.*
> *I'll love you for the rest of my life.*
> *On TV, you told me you loved me.*
> *I won't forget that.*
> *If you betray me…*
> *Oh, what a scary thought. So very scary.*
> *Because I would never betray you.*
>
> *From Someone You Know*

Yuma gulped.

What did all *that* mean?

Several letters from her fans arrived at her agency's office every day. Some letters were quite ardent, and some were nasty and harassing. But this message was not like those letters. Something was different about it. It was bizarre. And it felt all too real.

Maybe this is what had me feeling anxious earlier, she thought. A chill ran down her spine.

Yuma crumpled up the letter in her hand, envelope and all, and tossed it into the dustbin inside her entryway. Then she locked the door with both deadbolt and chain, and passed straight through her living room to her bedroom, where she burrowed into her full-size bed without stopping to remove her clothes.

She forced her eyes shut and pulled the duvet over her head.

Fortunately—or perhaps unfortunately—there was something she hadn't noticed.

The disturbing letter had been flecked with tiny bloodstains.

When Yuma entered the agency's meeting room, Bando and the other staff members were already at their seats around the table.

The sight of her manager's face reassured her more

than she would have expected. She sat in the chair next to him, leaned in to his ear, and spoke quietly. "I need to talk to you about something after the meeting. I got a strange letter yesterday..."

"A strange letter?" Bando's voice held a mix of curiosity and concern. But before Yuma could explain, he cut her off, saying, "We can talk about it later."

Bando cleared his throat, and the room went quiet as everyone turned their attention on him.

"I want to dive right in," he announced. "Today's theme is hop-skip-jump, Yuma! We're going to take this opportunity to re-examine our plans for her going forward. We've been fortunate that her poster campaign for Sanshin Denki has been a hit, and we can expect her to rise in popularity, as well. Her new single, 'Lariat of Love,' is debuting strong at number thirteen on the next Oricon chart. With everyone's hard work, I want to make this song an even bigger hit than her first single, 'Crossing Love.' I'd like to hear everyone's thoughts on how to promote her further. Let's have a lively discussion—all right, everyone?"

For the next hour, the team came up with numerous ideas to push Yuma's sales, several of which she thought had merit. In the end, however, the team settled on the uninspired approach of going forward with both her new Lolita look from the Sanshin Denki posters as well as her signature wild image. Yuma understood this as the typical indecisive result that came about when a group talked out ideas together.

They would begin by nurturing the popularity of the Sanshin campaign, playing up troubles with stolen posters (even if they had to fake a few thefts). At the same time, they would try to turn the microphone lasso move from "Lariat of Love" into a fad among the youth.

With a heavy yawn, Yuma stood up and went into the next room, where there was a kitchenette. She took a canister of instant coffee from the shelf and poured a scoopful into a paper cup, which she then filled with lukewarm water from a wall-mounted hot water dispenser. Without adding sugar or milk, she took a big gulp that left a grainy bitterness lingering on her tongue.

She retrieved a handkerchief from the rear pocket of her culottes and wiped the corners of her mouth. When she looked up, she saw Bando hurrying her way.

"Would you like me to make you some coffee?" she asked.

He nodded and sat on a folding chair at a small table, wiping sweat from his brow.

While she prepared his drink, Yuma said, "That meeting sure was pointless. We wasted all that time just to come up with the most obvious approach."

"Now Yuma-chan, you mustn't say that. Even if we end up with the most obvious plan, it carries more weight when arrived at by consensus. Just you wait and see. The team'll have better cohesion after that meeting."

The manager accepted the cup of coffee and began pouring copious amounts of sugar into the liquid. He dumped in four spoonfuls and then a fifth.

Now Yuma saw where his round belly came from. All that sugar intake had given his stomach the gentle rise of a Moomin character.

Showing her a confident smile, the manager said, "Just leave everything to me. I'm going to get 'Lariat of Love' into the top ten. You can count on it."

Mollified by his smile, Yuma said, "Thank you. I'll do everything I can, too. How should I start?"

"Primarily, I want you to take care of yourself," Bando said. "Your schedule is going to be packed with appearances and events all over the country. If you push yourself so far that you pass out, it'll all be for nothing. Your health needs to be your top priority."

He produced a notepad from his inside jacket pocket and began flipping through the pages so intensely Yuma almost laughed.

"Here's what your schedule was like as of yesterday," Bando said. "Tomorrow, you have a short event at Shoppers Plaza in Kyobashi, Osaka. The day after, you're in some of the surrounding cities—first a hand-shake event at a department store by Hirakata Station, and then in the evening, a guest appearance at a karaoke contest run by local businesses in Korien. That's it for those two days. Nothing too tough, there. But now that the whole team is on the same page, everyone will be working hard to fill in your schedule."

Bando downed his sugary coffee impatiently and sprang from his folding chair like there wasn't a minute to spare. He took two, then three steps toward the door before he stopped and belted out, "Oh, that's right. I almost forgot what I came in here for."

He returned to the metal chair and angled it to face Yuma. "You said there was something you needed to talk to me about. Something about a letter?"

When he said "letter," Yuma's body stiffened. Her eyes serious, she said, "Yes. A letter—a strange letter."

Seeing her expression, Bando sat up straight and listened.

Yuma opened her clutch bag and pulled out the crumpled note in question.

"This is it," she said. "It was so creepy, I threw it away right after I read it. But then I realized I wanted you to see it. So, here it is."

When Bando finished reading the letter, he tilted his head in thought and said, "Hmm. You're right, this is unusual—although, I do think it's probably just from a fan gone overboard."

"I probably shouldn't be scared, but I am," Yuma admitted. "I know it's just a letter. I can't quite explain what I'm feeling, but it's not good."

The idol looked over her shoulder. She thought she'd felt someone watching her.

"But Yuma," Bando said, "no matter how scary it might feel, it's just a letter, right? I've managed several idol singers now, so I know about this kind of thing. There's a lot of this sort of fan out there. With Asaka Ai, we got a letter that said, 'If I can't marry Ai, I'll kill myself.' But you know what? He never did. If you start worrying over what's in every single fan letter, there'll be no end to it."

Bando crumpled the letter back into a ball and tossed it into the wastebasket.

"Yuma-chan," the manager said cheerfully, "if you've got enough time to worry about something like this, I'd rather you worry about your promotional tour. To be perfectly frank, our future is riding on it."

Leaving the room, he stopped on the other side of the door and said, "If the person who wrote that letter tries to do anything to hurt you, I'll give my life to protect you. Don't you worry about it."

He gave her a smile and a wave.

Yuma wasn't entirely convinced, but she did feel a lot better.

For the fifth time that day, the man with the elephant eyes reached into the mailbox outside his room. Inside was a postcard ad for a loan shark business and several fliers for so-called "delivery health" call girl agencies. That was all he found.

He had gone to great efforts to find Yuma's apartment, and a week had passed since he delivered his letter. She should have replied by now. She should have replied days ago.

The man returned to his room and clicked his tongue in frustration.

Why hasn't she replied? Why?

He had poured his heart into his letter, so why hadn't she replied?

True, he hadn't written his name or address on the envelope. But the pair shared a soul bond. Signing it "From Someone You Know" should have been more than enough. And yet no reply had come.

The man asked himself, *Is she wrong for not sending me a letter? Or was I the one who did something wrong?*

No, he answered. *I didn't do anything wrong. And neither did Yuma. It wasn't either of us. Someone else must have interfered. That's the only answer.*

The man pulled a Yuma fan club magazine from his bookshelf. The self-published fanzine was called *Yukko Club*—Yukko being the fans' nickname for the singer. He opened the magazine and searched for the fan club's phone number.

Once he got what he needed from the magazine, he got out his notebook and looked at the schedule he'd compiled of Yuma's events.

Her next appearance was in Shoppers Plaza at Kyobashi. He narrowed his elephant eyes and made up his mind.

I'll meet Yuma in person, and I'll hear it straight from her mouth, with no one else to interfere. Then I'll know how she feels about me.

Yuma took the bullet train to Shin-Osaka Station, then by way of a couple local transfers, she reached Kyobashi Station. On the platform there, a group of male students recognized her.

She had done everything she could to blend in as an everyday woman, with her hair in a ponytail, her makeup easy and natural, and her eyes behind black-rimmed glasses. Most of her fans wouldn't have recognized her, but some of the particularly sharp-eyed students among the group had realized who she was, and they approached her, blabbering.

A pimple-faced junior high schooler slapped his friends on the back as he shouted, "See, I told you it was Kawasaki Yuma!"

A plump kid with silver-rimmed glasses stared at her agape and said, "It really is her!"

Another boy held out his right hand and said, "Would you shake my hand, please?"

Then, in the next instant, a number of the students thrust out their hands toward her.

In a manner that spoke to her familiarity with this kind of thing, she smiled for them and started to extend her arm to meet their handshakes. That was when Bando suddenly appeared from behind her, shouting, "No! No!"

He got in front of Yuma and spread his arms wide to keep the youths at bay.

He told them, "If you want to shake her hand, then come to the event space in Shoppers Plaza. If she does it special for you here, it wouldn't be fair to the other fans who are waiting."

The students glared at the balding interloper and hurled insults at him as they walked away.

"Why are you such a jerk?"

"Baldy!"

"I don't want her autograph anyway."

With a put-upon smile, Yuma looked to Bando and

said, "It was just a few handshakes. I don't mind."

"You can't be like that," he lectured. "Once you start indulging them, they'll just want more. Shake their hands, and they'll want autographs. Give them an autograph, and they'll want a picture with you. There's no end to a fan's desires."

He led her to the end of the platform, where a set of doors led into Shoppers Plaza. He ushered her through.

A few minutes later, the next train arrived at the platform. Office workers, men and women alike, crowded out from the train's doors. The platform was suddenly filled with people.

Lagging a little behind the throng, a single man was spat out from the train. With a slight stoop, he stood on the platform. He cleared his throat with a cough that could have come from a man twice his age. He spat out a gob of phlegm. If anyone had looked closely at him, they would have seen his unusually small, timid eyes.

It was him. It was the man with the elephant eyes.

A group of high school girls happened to be walking toward him as they chatted away about something or other. When he looked at them, his dark-skinned face turned a deep red. Quietly, he moved to the side of the platform so that they wouldn't look at him.

He must have been in a bit of a panic, because when he moved, something dropped from his pocket. He let out a small, stifled cry and quickly bent over and scooped up the object—a large box cutter.

After greeting the marketing and promotion staff of Shoppers Plaza, Yuma went to an impromptu green room set up for her in the company dormitory. The four-and-a-half tatami mats of the Japanese-style room were dotted with stains and smudges, lending the cozy space a lived-in feel.

While her manager was out of the room for a pre-event meeting, Yuma quickly got into her stage costume—a white blouse, cowhide vest, jean shorts, and a brown cowboy hat. It was her costume for "Lariat of Love."

The singer retrieved her microphone from her bag. She tested its weight in her hand and gave herself a moment to get re-accustomed to its feel.

Her manager had been the one to come up with the idea for throwing the mic like a lasso. Since Yuma had been in the baton twirling club in junior high, she learned the technique in short order. An idol without that experience would have taken years to perfect the move. Even still, despite already possessing the fundamentals, Yuma had needed to practice extremely hard before she had it down.

Several times, she had complained to Bando, "This

is pointless. I'll never get it."

Her third song, "Summer Love," ended with a move where she had to lift up the edge of her miniskirt and stick out her butt. When she started out performing that song, she cried and cried out of embarrassment and sadness, but learning this one was even harder. The lessons had taxed her, not only mentally, but physically as well.

When she saw "Lariat of Love" start rising up the Oricon chart, she felt truly happy. All her hard work was being rewarded.

Yuma returned the microphone to her bag. She let down her ponytail and brushed her hair all the way back. With the aid of the mirror over the sink, she applied a light layer of makeup. Now she was ready.

She plopped down on a floor cushion and waited for Bando to summon her.

Yuma made her entrance onto the small stage in Shoppers Plaza's event space.

There among the seats was the man. His eyes were surrounded with little wrinkles, just like those of an elephant. When he saw Yuma in her cowgirl costume, he whispered, "Ah. Now *this* is Yuma."

A trio of junior high school boys occupied the seats next to the man. They each unfolded one of those Sanshin Denki posters and waved them in the air.

Idiots, the man thought. *What's wrong with you people? You're just a bunch of perverts lusting after little girls.*

Filled to capacity with primarily middle and high-school-aged boys, the event space crackled with excitement. The man regarded the exuberant crowd with an annoyed glare.

They don't understand Yuma's true greatness, he thought. *I'm the only one who understands. I'm the only one for her!*

In an effort to restrain his agitated emotions, he reached into his pocket and squeezed the box cutter by its handle. The feeling of its cold metal against his skin calmed him, as if he were a babe and the knife were his mother's breast. The sensation of the metal traveled across his skin and through his body, reaching into the depths his mind.

The man smiled.

Without even realizing it, he stopped caring about the other fans around him. The only ones in the event hall were him and Yuma—at least that's how it felt, as his fantasy subsumed all other thoughts in his head.

When she finished singing "Lariat of Love," Yuma returned to her green room with sweat on her brow.

Bando was there waiting for her, a cold glass of soda

in hand. "You did great!" he said. "The crowd was really into it."

Yuma accepted the glass of soda and downed it in a single go. Her cheeks flushed in exhilaration, she said, "That was amazing. It was like a rock concert out there."

Bando said, "All that's left is the handshake session, and we'll be done here."

Yuma nodded deeply and wiped the sweat from her forehead with the sleeve of her blouse.

A little table and a cushioned folding chair waited on the stage. The set made for a rather dreary locale, but that was par for the course for these kinds of events.

Dressed in her street clothes, Yuma climbed the three or four steps to the stage, sat on the metal chair, and looked out at the room. It was the same as always.

The mostly teenaged boys who had been passionately waving their arms for her song now obediently sat in their seats waiting for the chance to shake hands with her.

To Yuma, it was beautiful, but at the same time, absurd. She couldn't help but let out a little chuckle.

The shrill-voiced woman emceeing the event announced, "We'll now begin the handshake session. Guests with tickets numbered one through ten, please line up at the stage."

The elephant-eyed man watched nothing but Yuma on the stage. He wondered how much it pained her to have to shake all those other men's hands.

But worry soon wormed its way into his fantasy. What if she was actually *enjoying* it? He needed to find out. He wanted to ask her, "You only shake those other men's hands because it's your job, right?"

What would he do if she answered, "I don't do it because it's my job. I do it because I like it."

As his mind worked through the scenario, he felt the blood drain from his face.

He struggled to remain in his seat. He couldn't bear to wait another minute without knowing how she felt. He pursed his lips. He clenched his teeth. He gnashed them so hard that his molars made a sound like they were crunching on leaves.

Yuma, please don't betray me. Please, please, you won't betray me, right?

He put his ticket back into his pocket, and his fingers brushed against the box cutter.

Yuma put emotion into each and every handshake. She held on to each fan for at least three seconds. She looked them in the eye and gave them a smile.

After around 150 handshakes, the effort started to tax her. Her hand didn't feel like a part of her anymore. It was like it was someone else's.

She looked out at the audience. Roughly half were still waiting. Though she kept reminding herself she should be thankful that all these people wanted to meet her, deep down she was so dreadfully sick of it.

His turn had finally come.

When he put his foot on the steps leading up to the stage, his entire body tingled. A single word came unbidden into his head: *destiny*.

This is my destiny.

He saw each step that brought him closer to Yuma as a step toward his destiny.

He climbed onto the stage, and Yuma was there, a few short meters away. For some reason, seeing his soul mate up close, he felt a little flustered. Just two, maybe three more steps, and they would be nearly touching.

His composure was faltering.

If this isn't fate, he asked himself, *then what is?*

With his eyes locked on to Yuma, he took one step, and then another, toward that which he believed was preordained.

Just then, Yuma felt a prickling pain in her chest. Lightly, she held her right hand over her heart where she felt the discomfort. It wasn't the pain of a physical wound or an illness. It was something more unusual.

A *premonition*, she thought in realization. *That's what this is—a premonition.*

As she kept on shaking the hands her fans offered to her, dread and that unfamiliar pain swelled in her chest. She understood that her body was trying to warn her on some primal level. Something sinister was drawing near. It was the same dread she had felt standing outside the entrance to her apartment building.

She looked into the face of the boy standing nervously in front of her. Was he the source of her distress?

When the elephant-eyed man saw he was now second in line, he felt a rush of energy springing up from somewhere deep within, like magma racing up an erupting volcano. But at the same time, he also felt a pain that was hard for him to place. It was something akin to shame, or maybe how a virgin bride might feel as she faced her wedding night.

He became suddenly embarrassed at the thought of Yuma looking upon his face and his appearance.

What will she think when she sees me? he asked himself. The thought made his body flush hot from head to toe in anxious embarrassment. He wasn't a handsome man. A dreadful worry sprang up from the depths of his mind. *What if she hates me?*

He ground his teeth, forward and back, like a chewing elephant. He felt as if sharp little pins were pricking into the backs of his eyes.

Oh, if only I were good-looking…

The thought hurt. It truly hurt.

How much pain I endure for you, Yuma.

He stared at her, unblinking.

You wouldn't betray a man who loves you as much as I do. You won't betray me, right?

Please, don't betray me!

For an instant, Yuma flinched.

The hand she was shaking felt oddly sticky.

The guy was probably sweaty—they often were—but his hand felt gummier than sweat usually did. It was almost like some kind of bodily fluid, and on top of that, he smelled vaguely like a wild animal.

Yuma pulled away her hand sharply. She looked at his face. His skin was darkish, rubbery, and creased like a tire tube. His dull eyes reminded her of an elephant, and they stared at her anxiously. His expression was lonesome, yet aggressive.

Could it be him…? Yuma wondered. Was he the source of her dread?

She turned her head to break away from his stare and said coldly, "Next in line."

When he faced Yuma, the man noticed her give him a signal.

She looked at him and nodded slightly.

At the time, he thought, *She really does know who I am.* He felt her message like it was an electric signal she transmitted directly into his brain. A long time ago, when he watched her on his television, she had sent him a message from beyond the curved glass tube: *I love you.* But now, at this short distance, the signal was all the stronger. It was too strong, in fact, distorting beyond recognition.

This isn't working, he thought. *I still can't tell what she's feeling.*

To ask her what she felt for him, he concentrated his own feelings and sent out a signal back to her. As their hands grasped, their passions manifested into sweat.

Is this sweat not my question manifested in form? And look, see how sweaty her hand is, too. Is that not her feelings for me, manifested in form? She loves me; that's why she sweats so.

With a satisfied smile, he thought, *Is this how passionate a woman can become for the man who loves her?*

He tightened his grip to say, *I love you.*

And that's when it happened.

Yuma suddenly broke away from his hand.

Then, as if she were speaking to a complete stranger, she said, "Next in line."

The man was stunned.

What? he thought. *Does she hate me?*

His grim fear returned to dominate his thoughts. A sound like an elephant's trumpet escaped his nostrils.

Yuma's gaze froze on the man with the elephant eyes.

As he stared back at her, his body began to visibly tremble.

Suddenly, without warning, the letter—that sinister letter—came to her mind.

Somewhere, beneath his animal stink, this man smells the same as the letter.

The elephant-eyed man fought to hold back the impulse bubbling up from deep inside and everywhere. Inside his pocket, he squeezed the box cutter as hard as he could, as he struggled to suppress a savage, violent urge.

Yuma sensed physical danger and stood reflexively. Bando came running from backstage.

Yuma's eyes locked onto the man's. She felt that something terrible would happen if she looked away.

Despair filled the man. He could read the mixture of terror and contempt in Yuma's eyes. Inside his pocket, he exposed the blade from its handle. His mind began to work like a computer circuit, racing down the branching paths of potential outcomes.

Do I stab Yuma with this box cutter? But then he thought, *If I stab her with this many people around, what will happen next? I'll be captured, arrested. I have to restrain myself for now and wait for my next chance.*

He turned his back to Yuma.

Somehow, Yuma carried out the handshake session to the very end. Exhausted, she leaned against Bando as he walked her into the green room. All she could think about was that man.

"Make sure he's not here," she said. Her frightened eyes darted into the shadows around the door.

"Make sure who's not here?" Bando asked.

"You know who I mean. The man with those elephant eyes, of course. He's not hiding on the other side of the door, is he?"

"Calm down, Yuma," he said as soothingly as he could. "Nso one can come here. The public isn't allowed in this area."

Yuma shook her head forcefully. "Not him. *He* could come here. Nothing is impossible for him." She squeezed Bando's hand. "He came to my apartment. Only you and I are supposed to know I live there. But he found it anyway."

Bando put his arm around her shoulders. "You're safe," he said. "Even if he managed to come here, he couldn't do anything with all the staff around. Besides, you don't even know if he's the same guy who wrote that letter."

Yuma nodded. But as she did, she thought to herself, *No matter what anyone else says, I know he wrote that letter. I know from his smell. And I know he'll come to me again...*

The man stood near the rear entrance to Shoppers Plaza. He took the box cutter from his pocket, blade exposed. He placed its cutting edge against his palm.

Yuma, he thought, *these are my feelings for you.*

He pulled the knife across his skin. Blood gushed out from the wound. Letting it pool in his hand, he approached a poster advertising Kawasaki Yuma's live performance and handshake session.

He reached for the poster and smeared his blood across the paper, as if instilling it with his feelings.

Beneath the film of red, Yuma smiled out at the world. He jabbed his pointer finger at her nose and said, "Yuma, this is the second time I've forgiven you. Please, I beg you, don't betray me again. This is the last time. You get no more chances after this."

Yuma dialed the phone number, partly resigned to the expectation he wouldn't answer. But, much to her surprise, this time he did.

"Yukio!" She spoke somewhat louder than she'd intended. Then, a bit peevishly, she said, "What's been going on? I keep calling you, and you're never there."

"Come on, don't be like that," Kawai Yukio protested. "You're the one who said not to call you so much because you'd be too busy with that new song."

"But, but…" Yuma waved the receiver, as if in denial. "But something really scary happened to me."

Like a cord stretched tight finally snapping under the strain, Yuma broke down crying.

Yukio said, "Yuma, it's all right. Look, we're talking now, aren't we?" With tenderness, he added, "If there's something bothering you, you can tell me about it."

"I…was so scared."

Between sobs, she told Yukio everything that had happened, from the letter to the man who had come to the handshake event.

Yukio was silent, and then he said, "That does sound strange. I have some pretty weird fans myself, and sometimes they'll send me their underwear or clippings of their hair—but I've never received a letter like that."

"Right? It's not normal. I think he's obsessed—he's crazy."

"I'm just not so sure of the connection between the letter and the man at the handshake session," Yukio said. "I think you might be too on edge, and you're overreacting."

"I'm telling you, it was him. I know it. No, I don't have any hard evidence. But I'm sure of it. He smelled the same as the letter."

"I feel like you're overthinking this," Yukio said, doubt evident in his voice. "Well, whatever the case, he hasn't done anything to hurt you so far, and he can't be shadowing you everywhere you go. Just be a little more cautious of what's around you, and I'm sure you won't have anything to worry about."

"He'll come," Yuma muttered.

"What did you say?" Yukio asked.

"He'll come. I know he will. He'll come to my apartment!" Shivering, she added, "Maybe he's already on his way here."

The next day, Yuma entered her agency's office and found Bando waiting for her with a fierce look on his face.

Full of cheer, Yuma asked, "Ban-chan, what's wrong?"

Bando had no smile for her. "What's wrong? What's wrong, you ask?"

He thrust a tabloid magazine at her and demanded, "What's this?"

It was one of those low-class, celebrity gossip rags.

"What about it?" Yuma said defensively as she took the magazine and began flipping through the pages. Halfway through, she found the photograph that had fouled Bando's mood.

The picture was of Yuma and Yukio together. It was from when they had snuck out on a date about a month ago. They were in a small, low-key snack bar, snuggled up to each other as they drank beer.

Who could have taken that picture? Yuma wondered in honest confusion. *There wasn't anyone in the bar who remotely looked like a photographer.*

"You sure made a mess of things," Bando said, "drinking with a man when you're underage. Even worse, you're going out with some C-grade idol, way beneath your level. If you're going to date someone, you'd better make sure it's a star. Then we'd have enough clout to keep pictures like this from surfacing."

Bando put his hands on his head, pushing his fingers through what little hair he had left. "The media will be all over this. They can't get enough of gossiping about popular idols. It'll probably be on TV within the week."

Feeling no sympathy, Yuma grew angry. "Look how worried you are, now. When I told you about that letter, you weren't bothered at all. You obviously care more about my CD sales than you care about me."

Bando glared at her. "Yes, your CD sales are important. But what I care about is for you not to become damaged goods. When these kinds of pictures go public, your fans are hurt the most. In the end, you're the one whose career is affected." He clicked his tongue in annoyance.

Somewhat concerned now, Yuma thought, *After climbing to the top five, "Lariat of Love" will start to slip back down—and my popularity might go down with it.*

She stepped toward Bando and clasped her hands around his. "I think it's going to be fine. These days, it's okay for idols to drink and go on dates. People appreciate honesty more than the fake innocent act. Don't worry. It'll all work out."

Bando shook his head slowly, then said, "Well, we can't take back what's already printed. Maybe you're right, and we'll get some publicity out of it." He let out a deep sigh. "You completely shut down the president of Sanshin Denki, but you'll date a cheap idol like this. Yuma, I don't think you were made for the entertainment world."

"Maybe I wasn't," Yuma said with a grin.

Bando returned her grin and joked, "You'd better watch out for the crazy fans. If they see this picture, they might lose it. Those fans can be scary sometimes."

He'd meant it just as a joke and nothing more. But Yuma didn't take it as one.

He's right, she thought. *Ban-chan is right. If that man sees this picture…*

For a second, everything seemed to go dark.

"I'll kill them! I'll kill them!"

At a tiny bookstore near the train station, the man stabbed a tabloid magazine again and again, shouting repeatedly. At the cash register, a female clerk averted her eyes from the spectacle. Apparently, she'd decided that ignoring him was the best way to ensure her own safety.

"I'll kill them! I don't know when, but I'll kill them!"

He'd slashed and shredded the picture in the magazine until the paper barely hung together.

The photograph was of Kawasaki Yuma and Kawai Yukio. Yukio had his arm around Yuma's shoulder.

Jealousy filled the man's heart, and his chest felt painfully tight. In that moment, his jealousy was so strong that he thought it might kill him. He resented that picture for making him feel this way. He resented the couple in the picture.

At some point, he began to cry; tears dripped down from his chin. He felt a burning sensation in his nose as salty snot began to stream out his nostrils. He felt sorry for himself. Why did he have to be hurt like this?

Suddenly, he looked up in realization. A glimmer came to his dull eyes, and he thought, *I'll tell Yuma.* He smiled. *I'll tell Yuma to break up with him. If I can just talk to her, she'll understand.*

But then he remembered how Yuma had looked at him during the handshake session. He pictured her expression of terror and contempt. Dejected, full of self-doubt, he turned his face down.

She might not understand. The thought struck fear into him. *What if she doesn't understand? What if she hates me?* He squeezed the box cutter's handle. *Then I won't have any other choice. I'll have to find strength in this blade. I'll have to turn to my last resort.*

Having found a new determination, the man was calm once more.

After finishing her recording for a TV talk show, Yuma took a taxi back to her apartment. She got out of the cab and looked around, as was her habit, to make sure no one had followed her home.

Seeing no one, she went in through the front entrance. The door wouldn't open for anyone without a matching key and number code. Thanks to the security system, the apartment provided complete safety. As long as she was here, she need not be afraid.

But that man had come inside. At least once, he had come.

Yuma exited the elevator and hurried to her door.

She shut it quickly behind her and engaged the lock, then the door chain.

It still wasn't enough to put her at ease. She ran to her phone and called Yukio. He didn't have any work tonight and when they had spoken earlier, he'd said that he would come over.

The answer machine picked up.

"Yukio, it's me," she said. Her voice was trembling. "Come over as soon as you get this message. I'm in my apartment. Please, come right away."

Her sixth sense was trying to get through to her. She could feel something—something beyond words. She sensed that something terrible was coming for her. It was getting close.

She thought she heard footsteps.

The doorbell rang. Yukio had come. Yuma unchained the door.

Yukio is here. She could think of nothing else. The sound of the doorbell had erased all fear.

As she opened the door, she pouted. "You're late. I've been waiting for—"

A man slid inside, through the open doorway.

It wasn't Yukio.

It was a man she didn't know.

She didn't know this man, but she'd seen him before.

Somewhere in her memories, he was there.

But who was he?

"You're Yuma-san," he said in a high-pitched voice, shrill enough to rattle the lid of hell itself. "You're Kawasaki Yuma-san."

The moment he had opened his mouth, her nose caught the smell. It was familiar. She knew, beyond any doubt, this was the man. This was the man who had filled her with terror at the handshake session. This was the man with those elephant eyes.

Her voice trembling, Yuma said, "Who are you? Why are you here?"

The man calmly locked the front door from the inside and moved the chain into place.

"I...I'm a huge fan," he said. He looked away in embarrassment. Even his ears had flushed red.

"If you're my fan," Yuma said as firmly as she could, "then come see me at a concert. This is my private space. It's not a place for fans to come."

That's right, she told herself. *He's your avid fan. You need to be strong with him.*

Staring him down, she ordered, "Now leave!"

The man's face turned an even deeper shade of red, but he said, "No. I won't leave."

He narrowed his elephant eyes, as if he were trying to bring something into focus. Then he retrieved a roll of brown packing tape and said, "I'm here because I'm going to ask you to do something."

Moving quickly, he circled behind Yuma's back. Without giving her a chance to escape, he wrapped his arms around her from behind.

"St-stop!" Yuma shouted as she flailed her legs, both of them bare below her short denim skirt.

The man bound her wrists with tape, pushed her onto her side, and straddled her body. Then he bound her ankles together, leaving her completely helpless.

He stood up and looked down at her, satisfied with his work.

"Yuma, I'll forgive every time you've wronged me before. But in exchange, I want you to sing only for me from now on."

She saw a crazed look in his eyes, and she knew she had to do something to escape him, or else.

Bound hand and foot, Yuma asked, "Why? Why are you tormenting me?"

The man's lips twisted into a frown. Stammering, he said, "You—you think I'm tormenting you? You've got it all wrong." His eyes rolled back so that only the whites showed. "I'm not tormenting you. I would never do that, no matter what happened."

He sounded like a child making excuses after his mother caught him doing something naughty.

Maybe that's how I can handle this, Yuma thought. *Whatever else he is, he's still a fan. He just might listen to me.*

She thrust out her wrists, wrapped in tape, and said firmly, "Then how do you explain this? You wouldn't call this tormenting me?"

The man's dark complexion slowly turned darker, and he began breathing roughly. "N-no—see, that's not to hurt you. B-but if… if I didn't do it, you'd run away." Keeping his head lowered, he looked at her with only his eyes. "And if you were to run way, I might not be able to control myself. I might do something we'd both regret."

Now his eyes entreated her to understand. "Sometimes," he explained, "I lose control of who I am. When I think about you betraying me, I sometimes lash out in violence." He gulped. "That's why… that's why…"

As he started to get flustered, he suddenly pictured that photograph of Yuma and Kawai Yukio. Yukio had his arm around her shoulders, and she was smiling, happy for the embrace.

A dark cloud of jealousy began to form, not just in his head or in his heart, but throughout his entire body. His hands shook, and a low rumble emanated from his throat. Then his small elephant eyes popped open so far they seemed they might fall out. He turned that widened gaze upon Yuma.

She sensed she was in danger. She curled her arms and legs like she was a shrimp and tried to wriggle away.

But in the next moment, he started slapping her face.

"How could you?" he shouted. "How could you look so sweet and be with... and be with someone like him?"

He grabbed her by her shoulder-length hair and lifted up her head, then shook her left and right.

Through grunts of pain, Yuma said, "St-stop it!"

But the man kept shaking her. His face took on a demonic look as he shouted, "How about this?! How about this?!"

"St-stop..."

Then with a little snapping sound, a few dozen of her hairs pulled loose. The strands clung to his fingers.

Yuma's head dropped to the carpet. She remained still, frozen from the pain and terror. Some moments later, she heard the man sobbing. She cracked open her eyelids and saw him holding his head in his hands. Her hair was still stuck to his fingers.

"Forgive me," he said. "Please forgive me. I didn't mean to do that..."

Fat tears spilled from his small, ugly eyes. He looked at her with those watery eyes, and their gazes met.

"Y-Yuma-chan. I'm sorry. But... but it's your fault. That happened because of the way you've been acting. You must never meet with that man again."

Pushing through the pain in her face and her head, Yuma looked up at him. "All right. I won't see him again. So please, take off this tape."

The man bobbed his head in approval and began to slowly pull apart the stubborn tape. As he worked at it, he said, "Thank you, Yuma. Thank you for forgiving me. Thank you." He began to cry again, but this time with tears of admiration and relief.

"But Yuma," he added, "I'm just going to come out and say it. Just because you're free to move again, don't think you can run away. If you try to run, this is going to get scary."

"Of course I won't run," Yuma said, as she eyed the distance between herself and the door. "I wouldn't even think of it."

She felt she could outrun him, at least with a head start. Freedom was not far away—just across the living room, through the front hall and out the door, then down the emergency stairway.

The problem was the door chain. She worried that he might catch her while she stopped to undo the lock. No outcome could be worse. He'd bind her with that packing tape again, and she'd be completely helpless. If only he'd remove his attention from her for just one minute, maybe two. Then she could have time to unlock the door and escape.

The man was laughing.

"I'm so happy," he said, taking her hands in his. "You're right here in front of me. Not a poster or a picture, but the real Yuma." He pulled her hands quickly toward him, and the momentum carried her body after them, so that she leaned against him. A cold chill ran through her.

I would rather die than be held by him, Yuma thought, and meant it.

He put his arms around her and looked her up and down, fire in his eyes. The edges of his lips began to twitch. He clenched his fists so hard they trembled. He seemed to be trying, through great effort, to contain the lustful feelings that had come over him.

"Yuma is an idol," he muttered to himself, but this close, Yuma heard every word. "She's a cute, adorable idol. We can't have sex, no matter how much I want to. Oh, how much I want to. But we can't…"

His eyes burned with an animal lust as he gazed at her face, then her neck, then her breasts.

He exhaled deeply.

He pressed his hands against his chest.

"We can't!" he cried. "We can't. We can't have sex!"

He unzipped his jeans and pulled out the ugly thing that had swollen and risen between his legs. The unwashed smell quickly invaded the air around them.

"Yuma," he said, "you mustn't watch this. We can't have sex, so I have to do this instead."

He turned his back to her and began stroking himself. His shoulders rose up and down, and his breathing became heavy.

For a moment, Yuma watched in stunned silence as the carnal scene unfolded. She had never seen a man do what he was doing, let alone a man such as him. His body began to shake, as if a spirit had possessed him. He seemed to be building toward climax. His back curled, and his hand began to quicken.

Calmly, Yuma thought through her situation. *It'll probably take him another two minutes or so to finish. This might be my chance to escape.* Out of the corner of her eye, she watched the man, rapt in his act of self-pleasure. Slowly, careful not to make any noise, she began walking. Leaving faint depressions on the carpet, she walked toward the front hallway. *Please don't finish yet,* she prayed. *Take it nice and slow. Enjoy yourself.*

Reaching the front door, she looked over her shoulder to make sure his attention remained occupied.

She could hear him moaning now.

Good. He was still going.

Yuma reached for the door chain. Her gut was screaming at her to hurry, but she took her time, making sure not to raise the slightest noise.

She put her hand on the doorknob. When she turned it, the door opened with a *click*.

I made it! she thought, as the path to liberty presented itself before her. She took her first step into the freedom for which she yearned. But she couldn't take a second step. Something incredibly strong pulled her back inside.

It was him. He grabbed her with one hand on her shoulder. He spun her to face him. Their eyes met. He looked more elephant than man.

With his other hand still in between his legs, he howled.

At the same time as she screamed, the man finished.

"I told you," he said, stroking Yuma's hair.

She cried, shaking her head.

The man sat cross-legged, having placed her across his lap. She'd tried to struggle, but he was stronger than he looked, and she hadn't been able to pry herself free.

Giving it everything she had, Yuma pleaded, "Forgive me. I won't run away anymore…"

The man regarded her with sadness in his eyes. "No, you'll run. I wish I could believe you, but you'll run."

The man withdrew a box cutter from his pocket. He pushed out the blade, and it *click-click-clicked* its way through the notches built into the handle. Yuma knew what that sound meant.

"No! Stop!" she screamed, before panic turned her words unintelligible. There was no doubt over what he was about to do. If she didn't escape, he was going to stab her.

As she flailed about, he held her in place with his other hand.

She opened her mouth wide and bit down on his inner thigh. The bitter taste of his denim jeans filled her mouth.

"That won't work," he said. "I'm not stopping. All right, Yuma—are you ready?"

His face emotionless, he pushed the box cutter's blade into the bottom of her foot. Sharp pain shot all the way up to her brain. When she screamed, her voice sounded nothing like that of an idol, but like an old woman being strangled, on the verge of death.

The man said, "Yuma, you're just going to have to endure this. Just a little longer, okay?"

He swung the box cutter again and again into the bottoms of her feet. Blood gushed freely from the gashes. By the time he was done, she was too weak to even cry out.

He looked at her ruined feet. With disgust in his voice, he muttered, "You won't be able to run from me anymore. You have to accept it now. You're going to stay right here and sing for no one but me."

Yuma opened her eyes with a start. She awoke to a throbbing pain in her feet. She must have fallen unconscious, but for how long she didn't know. She looked down at her feet and saw that they had been wrapped with a towel, now stained through with red.

Coming to grips with the pain, she looked around the room. The man wasn't anywhere to be seen. He might have been in the living room, but she heard nothing from that direction. The door chain was still unlocked. If she could only crawl that way…

She put a little weight on her feet and was immediately met by a stab of incredible pain. She wasn't going anywhere.

Maybe someone will come rescue me. She thought of Yukio. *That's right, I have Yukio. As soon as he hears the message I left him, he'll come.*

She felt the blood return to her face. She repeated the thought, trying to make herself believe it—trying to will it to be true. *As soon as he hears my message, he'll come right away. Yukio, come quickly! Come right now!*

She clasped her hands in prayer and stared at the door. *Come before that demon returns.*

Then, as if someone had answered her prayer, the doorbell rang. She heard a key slide into the lock.

It's Yukio. Yukio came for me.

Yuma sat up, anticipating his rescue. The knob

turned, and the door swung open.

"Yukio!" Yuma cried.

This time, it really was him. Kawai Yukio stood on the other side of the door.

When he saw her there on the floor, blood on her feet, his expression filled with shocked disbelief. And then he stepped inside.

"What happened to you?" he said.

Or rather, that was what he started to say. About when he said, "What happened," a figure silently appeared out of hiding. Before anything else could occur, the man slashed Yukio's throat with the box cutter.

Air burbled unnaturally out from Yukio's throat as he collapsed on the spot. When his face struck the carpet with a clap, the wound on his throat split open wide and blood exploded out like fireworks.

The man casually tossed aside the box cutter and said, "That's what you get!"

"Yukio!" Yuma cried out. Oblivious to her pain, she crawled to the front door, where she cradled her lover's head in her arms. From the single line that had been drawn across his throat, the blood kept coming out in little spurts.

He had died almost instantly.

Having witnessed the death of the man she loved most, a new emotion sprouted deep inside her. She wanted to kill the man who did it.

Then, that very man pulled Yukio from her arms and tossed him into the bathroom like so much garbage into the can. Yuma picked up the discarded box cutter at her feet and turned a hate-filled stare at the man. He noticed her looking at him and approached her with his arms spread wide.

"What's wrong, Yuma? I just took care of a man who was pestering you. He tried to spoil things between us, and I punished him for it. You promised you weren't going to see him again, didn't you? You should look happier to be rid of him. Give me a smile."

Yuma shook her head. "You despicable monster. *You're* the one I want dead!"

The man was taken aback. "Wh-what did you say?" The veins on his temples stood out. "I'm doing everything I can for you, and you say you want me dead?"

He glared at her. All sense of self-control vanished from his eyes. And then, with incredible speed, he rushed toward her. He yelled, "Before I do anything else, I'm going to make you pay!"

She gripped the box cutter tightly in both hands. She lifted the blade high above her head.

The man, roaring like a wild animal, was nearly upon her.

She swung the box cutter at the top of his shoulder. The blade dug into his shoulder blade and slid down at an angle, shaving off a centimeter-long patch of flesh. She had swung with so much force that the leftover momentum sent her staggering forward a couple steps.

The man held his hand over the wound as the blood came gushing out. "Yuma!" he shouted. His eyes clouded with a cold, shark-like fury. "Yuma! What have you done? You really mean to kill me?"

Blood seeped through his fingers and trickled down his arm. Yuma renewed her grip on the box cutter and glared at the man.

"Don't come any closer," she said. "I'll kill you. I-I mean it."

Standing on one knee, she held the weapon in front of her. The edge of her short skirt lifted, revealing a glimpse of her underwear.

The man's lips twisted into an ominous grin. "You'll kill me, you say? You would kill a man who loves you as much as I love you?" Locking his eyes on hers, he slowly approached her. "Do you really think that little body of yours is capable of killing me?"

The anger vanished from his eyes. In its place came the look of a vulture seeking its prey. He let out an eerie, birdlike cry and charged in to tackle her.

As he ran at her, she brought the box cutter down with her full strength behind it. The blade's tip sunk into his back. A good hit, but—

The man only grunted.

He kept coming, grappling with her. He took hold of her waist with both hands and threw all his weight upon her.

The smell of sour meat assaulted her nostrils. His flabby body reminded her of a waterbed she'd tried out on a TV show once. His bulk sunk in around her. She flailed her arms and legs, but he didn't budge.

"You smell nice," he said. "So, this is your smell. It's delightful."

The man buried his face in Yuma's chest and breathed in deeply. His stubble scratched around the tips of her breasts. The sensation was so disgusting that it nearly caused her to black out.

"I won't restrain myself any longer," he said. "There's no turning back for us now. No matter what I do, you'll always hate me. It's better for me to act on my true feelings."

He pulled down her blouse and bra, then brought his lips near her exposed breasts.

"So th-these are your breasts…"

He put her nipple into his mouth and roughly began to suck.

"Stop! Stop!" she cried.

Caring nothing for her protests, he sucked at her nipple so hard that it felt like he might tear it off. The man's breathing became rougher, and he drew his waist in closer to her. She felt his stiffness against her thigh. For the first time in her life, Yuma cursed herself. She cursed everything that had led her to this moment.

Why did this have to happen to me? What did I do to deserve this? Is it just because I'm an idol?

Even as she gagged at the stench of his body odor, she reached around him and pulled the box cutter from his back.

His fingertips slithered up through the bottom of her skirt, where they impatiently tugged at the edges of her panties. His crooked fingers pressed against her most sensitive area.

Just then, Yuma stabbed the box cutter into his upper arm. The blade sliced through the surrounding fat and mangled the muscles beneath, and she learned that even this monster could screech in pain.

But then, he slapped her with incredible force. The impact was so strong, she felt like it might break her face, but she refused to let go of the box cutter.

"Damn you," he snarled. "Look what happens when I go too easy on you. You start getting ideas."

Greasy sweat beaded on his skin as he bore through the pain. He stepped over her and stomped his foot down on her chest. The wind rushed out of her lungs and escaped her lips in a bubbly mix of air and spittle.

Yuma cursed him silently, senselessly swinging the box cutter, slicing across his legs over and over.

The man grunted and put his hand to his ankles. "I can't move my foot," he said tearfully. "I... I can't move it."

Those wild slashes must have shredded the Achilles tendon of his left leg.

Now we're in the same position, Yuma thought. She formed a tight-lipped smile as if to say, *That's what you get.*

Wriggling her body like a snake, she shifted herself over to the side of the hallway. Following the wall, she crawled like an inchworm, pulling herself toward the front door. She moved even slower than she had thought possible. Her legs were nearly useless. She had to drag herself with only the strength in her arms and hips. Drawing on every energy reserve she had, she advanced—however gradually—toward the door. She didn't look back over her shoulder, only forward, ever forward.

Holding his hands against ankles that wouldn't stop bleeding, he looked toward her and said, "Whatever I have to do, Yuma, I'm not letting you escape."

Yuma nudged the half-open door with her head, creating enough space for her to pass through, into the outside hallway. She turned toward the elevator and willed strength into her leaden arms. She was not all that muscular to begin with, and the fierce fighting had exhausted her limbs to the point of numbness.

And then, she couldn't move them anymore. She tried to reach for the handrail that ran down the hall, but she couldn't lift her arm. Her body was overcome by total exhaustion.

I need to rest, she told herself. With one final effort, she sat up and leaned her back against the railing, to give her body the respite it needed. Sitting there, slumped against the wall outside her apartment unit, she looked out the window and saw several stars twinkling in the sky.

Night had fallen without her knowing it. Cars honked their horns in the distance. A cool wind comforted her weary body. She heard what sounded like a nighttime baseball game coming from a TV on an upper floor.

Yuma felt keenly aware of the irony around her. Just a tiny distance away waited a wide-open world where she could be the idol Kawasaki Yuma, living in pampered comfort and basking in admiration. But here, in these confines, she was trapped in hell. Hades had Cerberus, but this hell had its own, even more relentless, jailer.

Why... why does everything have to be so tragic?

As she gazed at the twinkling stars, she began to weep.

But reality was not going to allow her any time for sentimentality.

Her apartment door opened like a creaking coffin, and the man's head peered out from within. His head snapped in her direction. "There you are," he said with a smile.

Yuma put her head in her hands and said, "No more, no more…"

But then, forcing her arms to move again, she began crawling to the elevator.

With only the use of his left arm and right leg, the man emerged into the hallway and came after her. Reaching the elevator, Yuma stretched out her arm to press the call button. But the man was already upon her. His hand closed around her calf.

"I've caught you, Yuma," he said. He clamped his fingers down hard, and the pressure rekindled the pain from the wounds on her feet. "Even if you kill me, I'm never letting go."

His grimy fingernails dug into her skin.

Yuma gave up on the elevator. She turned her body toward the emergency stairway. With the man's fingers digging into her, it would take an extreme measure to free herself of his grasp.

Then an extreme measure is what I'll take.

She threw herself rolling down the stairs. The sudden force caused the man to lose his grip. His nails tore off little strips of flesh from her calf, but at least she was free.

Yuma tumbled down to the landing where the staircase doubled back, halfway between stories. Her head slammed against the concrete, but she ignored the pain as she turned herself to roll down to the next floor. Once she made it there, she'd call for help as loud as she could. Maybe then she could be set free from this hell.

But cold, merciless reality came to shatter such hopes. When she looked down the stairs, she saw the fire door was shut, sealing any hope of escaping that way behind it. Faced with this dead end, she looked up the stairs from where she'd come. The man was looking back down at her.

"Yuma," he shouted. "I'm coming!"

"You're what?" she shouted reflexively in confusion.

The next moment, he was sailing through the air like a pro wrestler diving from the top rope. If he landed on her with his full weight, he might crush her to death.

Pushing with her head, she arched her neck and lifted her shoulders from the ground. She rolled to the side.

His soft landing taken from him, the man slammed into the concrete with a loud crunching sound and crumpled into a heap.

But he was still breathing, moaning in pain. He started to rise, shaking. He was still alive.

Yuma looked at her hands. There, forgotten but still held in her right hand, was the box cutter.

She looked to the man's face. Blood streamed down

his forehead. Pain had twisted his countenance into a grimace. His eyes were teary, pleading her for help.

As she watched this man who had taken so much from her, and caused her so much pain, she was overcome with a feeling that she could not define.

"Goodbye," she said. "We'll never meet again."

She pushed the box cutter deep into his right eye.

She tumbled in through the open door of her apartment and immediately felt ill. Stomach juices began pushing their way up, bringing their acidic taste to the back of her mouth. The cuts on the bottoms of her feet hurt even more than they had before. She brought her hand to her head, and everywhere she touched, her fingers were met by cutting pain. Scratches and scrapes covered her arms and legs. Her blouse was open, and her bra was exposed.

Looking back on it, she'd been through an incredible fight.

Dragging her legs behind her, she crawled into her living room. She began to weep.

I'm safe, she thought. As she crawled she let herself cry. After some time, she looked up bleary-eyed and thought, *My manager — I need to call him.*

Rather than dial 110 — the emergency number for the police — her first thought was of calling her manager.

With great effort, she sat up and stretched out her arm toward the telephone in front of her. The fight had left her weak, and she struggled to reach it. Finally, just as her fingertips landed on the receiver, she felt a strange pressure on her leg.

Something sticky pressed down on her skin. She turned her head to look over her shoulder. What she saw was totally red.

What is that? She tilted her head in confusion. Her mind couldn't unpack what her eyes were seeing. It looked like some red thing reaching out a tentacle to grab her leg.

No, not a tentacle. It was an arm. A red-painted human arm.

It had to be…

Yuma thought for a moment. Then the answer came to her. When it did, she laughed. But as she laughed, her face gradually froze.

"No! No more!" she cried in a deep, shoulder-heaving scream.

Answering her scream, the red thing whispered, "Yuma…"

There was no denying it anymore. It was the man. It was the man she'd thought dead.

She didn't want to believe it. She didn't want to, but it was him. As proof, the box cutter she'd stabbed into his eye was still there, standing straight out from the socket.

The now one-eyed man muttered under his breath as he pulled her ankle toward him. Flailing with her entire body, she managed to shake free from his grasp. She crawled away from him, her arms bent like a cricket's.

She couldn't make her legs push. She could hardly move her body at all. But she kept pushing herself ever forward, propelled by terror. The man crawled after her, much in the same way, using his arm alone.

"Yuma, it's me," came the hoarse voice from behind. "It's me…"

Hearing him speak, she felt her body begin to give up what little strength it had left.

"Please Yuma, don't go. Wait for me. I want to die with you. We'll go to heaven together."

Yuma summoned every last shred of willpower she had and used it to keep fleeing from the voice.

But even that willpower was beginning to weaken.

What good will running do? Where can I go?

Ahead of her was a sliding glass door. On the other side, a balcony. Beyond that, only death. Flinging herself over that railing would bring her certain death.

Acting only on unconscious instinct, Yuma slid open the glass door and exited onto the balcony. There, she put her hands on the railing and turned herself around to face her enemy.

The man was only a few meters away.

Crawling on his stomach, he raised his head like a snake to look at her. He kept on staring, with the box cutter protruding from his eye and his face painted red with blood. His mouth dropped open, and he gave her a broad, happy smile.

"Yuma, we're going to die together. Not alone. That makes me so happy, Yuma." He stuck out a purple-tinged tongue and licked the blood from around his lips. "Tell me, how would you like to die? You probably want it painless, I bet."

He slithered one step forward and asked, "How does strangling sound?" Another slithering step. "We could both jump off the balcony." Another step.

She shook her head, *No, no.* She didn't want to die. More than that, she didn't want to be killed by this man. Trying to put what distance she could between herself and him, she kept her back against the railing and sidled to the right.

The man's head turned, locked on to her, as he pulled himself forward with his arm. Backed into the corner of the balcony, Yuma now truly had nowhere left to go.

The man stared at her, savoring the moment. "You really are pretty, Yuma. You're so cute when you're scared. You see now—you have nowhere left to run."

He was now two meters away.

"You know, now that I think about it," he said, "I think I'd rather kill you with the box cutter, after all. It will hurt some, but you'll just have to endure it." He put his hand to the box cutter embedded in his eye. "Besides, I've endured so much pain for you already."

He pulled out the knife. With a messy, wet sound, a jelly-like object came out with the blade. Countless thin tendrils hung down from it.

It was his eyeball.

Fresh blood gushed out from the empty cavern of his eye socket.

"It hurts, Yuma. Oh, my eye *really* hurts." He shook his head again and again. Then he adjusted his grip on the box cutter. "But this pain doesn't even compare to how much it hurt when I learned you were seeing another man."

As if with the last of his strength, the man sat up, and then stood. Severed Achilles tendon or not, he stood.

"Yuma, it won't be much longer now. First, I'm going to stab this into your eye. And then your throat. And finally, your heart."

The man aimed the tip of the box cutter at Yuma and rushed toward her.

With her back to the railing, Yuma had nowhere left to run. One word filled her thoughts. *Death.*

Her arms and legs trembled. She wet herself. As if her body had crumbled beneath her waist, she slumped to the floor. Her rear landed first, followed by her hands.

What? Her hand had landed on something hard. She grabbed it instinctively, recognizing the feel of the object immediately. *My...microphone.* She had used this microphone to practice her final move for "Lariat of Love."

Her thoughts flooded with memories of the long hours spent practicing in her apartment.

It was so tough. I worked so hard to learn that. That's why... that's why...

She looked up. The man's deep red face was before her eyes. The box cutter was almost upon her. Only the shortest of distances stood between her and death. She had no more time.

"I'll give you your wish!" she shouted.

For a moment, the man hesitated.

"I'll sing for you," Yuma said. "I'll sing only for you." Her hand tightened around the mic. The lyrics replayed in her head:

> *I'll snare you with my burning love.*
> *Oh, my lariat of love.*

She threw the microphone.

At nearly the same time, the man swung the box cutter.

Cable in tow, the microphone brushed past the knife and went winding around and around the man's neck.

Yuma twisted her body to the side, avoiding the descending blade and then yanked on the cable, putting all her weight behind it.

The cable went taut, and the sound of snapping neck bones rang out flatly. The man let out one last grunt before collapsing on the spot. For a second, his body rattled violently. And then he was still. His face puffed out like that of a drowned corpse, and a purple hue began to show through his dark skin.

I did it!

Yuma had won. She had defeated the monster. As her consciousness finally began to succumb to exhaustion, she knew she had won.

On the verge of passing out, she began reeling the microphone in by its cable. The mic slowly unwrapped from the man's neck and returned to her. By the time she had it tightly in her grasp, she was on the verge of losing consciousness.

She held the microphone like a pistol and pointed it at the fallen man. In the last moment before passing out, a voice shouted inside her, victorious.

Bang!

3

EVEN WHEN I EMBRACE YOU

◇

THE RAIN FELL WITHOUT END—not just any rain, but a gloomy downpour, tinged with acidity. Moist air seeped in through the thin wooden walls of the man's room. As it settled over his skin, he felt as if the wetness would rot him to his core.

I can't take this any longer, the man thought sourly, wiping the sweat from his forehead with a kitchen rag. He set the rag down on the table in front of him, and then leaned down and pulled out a cardboard box sitting on the floor underneath.

The box was stuffed with large wads of grimy cloth—former bedsheets, possibly. The man pushed aside the bunched-up fabric and dug out an object that just about filled his arms. He looked at the object for a moment, lifted it up to his face, then slipped it over his head.

The pungent odor of mildew struck his nostrils. The inside of the thing was so oppressively stifling that he nearly choked. The musty, stale air mingled with his exhaled carbon dioxide and, with nowhere else to go, lingered in a cloud around his face. The only ventilation came through a small rectangular opening, barely the size of his closed lips, located partway between his eyes and his nose. The opening also served as his only window to see out from within. In truth, the slit so severely restricted his field of view that he may as well have been blind. As long as the object was over his head, moving and acting freely would only be possible with great difficulty.

He kept the thing on for a while as he stood in place, muttering, "I need to get used to wearing this, as if it were a part of my own body. But there isn't time. There just isn't time. I have to do something. I *have* to..."

With hesitant steps, he staggered his way over to the wall and stood in front of his calendar.

"Damn it!" The man removed the object from his head. Without thinking, he threw it with both hands against the floor. It bounced a few times and rolled to a wobbling stop.

The man's face was drenched with sweat, and he took in deep, shoulder-heaving breaths. His dead eyes stared at the calendar with such intensity that he could have bored a hole into it.

A large X had been marked over the square for the twenty-sixth of September.

"Only one week left," he said. "I'm nearly out of time." His voice rose as he repeated, "I don't have enough time. I don't have enough time!"

Enough time for what?

His expression twisted into something sinister. His lips were taut and curled, trembling. His eyes, unfocused, stared off into nowhere.

The man balled his fists. He squeezed them tight and then tighter still, his joints creaking. Blood began to seep between his fingers as his nails dug into flesh. He didn't know what it was that hastened him with such urgency. All he knew was that he felt a deep-set irritation, clawing at him from within.

He opened his bloody fists and rubbed them across his face, painting it in deep red. For a moment, he seemed to be smiling. Then a sorrowful wail escaped his throat. His voice was shrill, like some strange bird's call. It sliced through the stagnant air, pierced the thin walls, and melded into the expanse of black, low-hanging storm clouds.

I'm happy, right? Yukiko thought. *I'm supposed to be happy.*

She picked up the weekly men's magazine in front of her. The periodical led with pin-up pages featuring Yukiko herself, wearing a natural, no-makeup look with just a subtle hint of lipstick. Behind her was a quiet, wintry outdoor landscape, snow falling all around.

The scene was appropriate, and not just because of her given name, which had the word "snow" in it. The caption leading her featured section read, "In this winter for idols"—which referred to the slump in popularity pop idols were experiencing—"a single flower blooms from the snow."

Indeed, Tsukioka Yukiko was a traditional kind of pop idol rarely seen in recent times.

How could I not be happy to receive so much attention so quickly after my debut?

Yukiko had never aspired to become an idol singer. She'd always had an interest in becoming an entertainer, but being an idol was never her one and only dream. When she graduated from high school, she had found herself without direction. She was friends with a model, and on a whim, she joined the same modeling agency that represented her friend. Yukiko viewed it as little more than just a part-time job to get her by until something else came along.

That wasn't to say she did it with no reason whatsoever. Modeling offered substantially better pay than waitressing at some family restaurant or café, and she'd always liked the idea of being famous, even if the desire had never defined her. It was with that level of thought—and a few small pushes from her friend—that Yukiko entered the modeling world.

Yukiko was not particularly glamorous, but her face had a traditional beauty, and gigs came in at a fairly brisk pace. After a little while, the agency's owner asked her if she wanted to give Tokyo a try. Apparently one of his business acquaintances at a talent agency there had expressed interest in her. He wanted to represent her, cultivate her career.

Yukiko took up the offer without hesitation.

For the first six months in Tokyo, she lived under her new boss's roof and spent all day, every day, in intense lessons. She threw herself into her vocal training and jazz dance lessons, even if the exact nature and direction of her debut remained unclear.

She still hadn't figured out what she wanted to be, but from the content of her studies, she began to suspect her new boss intended for her to become a singer. When he started bringing songwriter-types to observe her vocal lessons, Yukiko was sure of it.

Even now, she could still remember being mystified by her boss's choice, as she knew she lacked vocal talent. Nevertheless, she ended up debuting as a pop idol of the traditional, innocent style that didn't demand that much singing ability. That too felt like a mismatch to her, as she didn't consider herself innocent, either.

Meanwhile, the media was saying that pop idols were in their winter. Privately, Yukiko questioned the sense in having her debut as an idol just as they were going out of fashion—but she kept such complaints to herself. She wanted to be in entertainment, and she was. If her manager decided she would be an innocent idol, then that was the path she would follow.

And yet her doubts continued. She was too old to be an idol. Her personality was demure and old-fashioned, whereas the younger girls were more lively and dynamic. She had been certain no one would buy her music.

But, contrary to her expectations, she found an audience.

Her debut single, "Flower in the Snow," was a smash hit, selling tens of thousands of CDs. After an appearance in a soft drink commercial, her name was on everybody's lips. (Her only line, spoken softly: "Refreshingly pure.") Within six months of her debut, she had established herself as one of the top idol singers.

Her outmoded style meant she had no direct rivals worth mentioning, and perhaps being out of step with the trends served to make people take notice of her rather than ignore another face in the crowd. Whatever the causes may have been, in a remarkably short time, Tsukioka Yukiko succeeded in leaving her own mark on the music industry.

Debuting as an idol was itself an accomplishment, and in the entertainment world, where many careers were over before they even began—buds sprouting, never to blossom—Yukiko had secured real popularity and fame. It should have been enough to make her more than happy.

If I'd wanted to become an idol from the start, she thought, *I'd be up in the clouds right now.* In her mind, she stuck a scolding tongue out at herself. *What will ever be enough for me?*

Having finished an appearance on an FM radio program in Tokyo's Akasaka district, Yukiko took a late lunch at a nearby restaurant. Sitting across from her, her manager Domoto Yoriko was intensely focused on a plate of spaghetti carbonara. Something about the seriousness of the woman's expression as she conveyed the pasta to her mouth made Yukiko giggle quietly.

Yoriko was thirty-three and single. She wore her hair pulled back and had silver-rimmed glasses.

She looks just like Fräulein Rottenmeier, she thought, picturing the strict governess from *Heidi, Girl of the Alps.* Now Yukiko chortled outright.

Yoriko looked over the rims of her glasses with an expression that only made her look even more like Fräulein. "You should hurry up and eat," she said, twirling her fork to pick up the next bite. "We only have time for a short lunch before you're due at Marusho."

Yukiko's expression turned sullen, and she pouted. "Do I absolutely *have* to go to that department store? The exhibition starts tomorrow. Why can't I just show up then?"

"What are you talking about? You know how extremely important this event is for you. The whole exhibit is about you—you're the star." Yoriko sighed, and began reminding Yukiko, in exhaustive detail, of all the hard work she had put into organizing the event.

The last idol the department store had held an exhibition for had been Matsuda Seiko, and that was fifteen years ago. Yukiko was grateful for everything her manager had done to make the exhibition happen, but she'd heard this speech a hundred times.

When Yoriko was finished, the manager added, "That's why I want you to look over the displays for yourself. You need to see, with your own eyes, how it all came together."

Yukiko replied, "All right, all right," then puffed out her cheeks.

The Marusho department store had a long and successful history, in part due to its location adjacent to a major Tokyo transit hub. The passing years had inevitably begun to show their wear, but the building had a distinctive character that retained its appeal.

Yukiko and Yoriko went in through the employees' back entrance. The receptionist called for the exhibit's coordinator, who came to usher them up to the event space on the twenty-fifth floor where the singer's exhibit was installed.

The coordinator was a man in his fifties, and as the group waited inside the elevator, he passed a hand through his thinning hair. Proudly, he said, "I shouldn't be one to brag, but this turned out really well—especially the life-size figure of Tsukioka-san. It's not just your ordinary wax statue."

Yukiko smiled pleasantly at the man, but on the inside, the whole thing repulsed her. The exhibit was meant to put the singer on full and open display, and the items included her actual toothbrush and coffee cups. She found it absolutely creepy. Any fans that would delight in seeing her personal belongings like this were not fans she wanted to have.

Worst of all was that life-size figure of herself. Apparently, some superfan had spent three months sculpting the piece, but she had no desire to see a replica of herself—and she got chills when she thought of her copy being put on display in full view of who knew how many people.

The elevator doors opened, and the exhibit's coordinator gave a deep bow before spreading his arms wide as if to say, *Well? What do you think?*

The entrance to the exhibit space was directly outside the elevator. It was a large space, big enough to fit a comfortable home inside. The walls and floors were clean and polished, and the exhibit was brightly lit, with spotlights on the various showcases and displays adding tasteful and eye-catching splashes of color.

One display featured photographs taken of her lessons before her debut, alongside the leotard she wore for her jazz dance practice and a smartly arranged assortment of other objects from that time.

Yukiko was impressed. This wasn't the haphazard and chaotic mishmash she'd pictured. A four-sided standing display case occupied the center of the first viewing room. Inside the showcase were her various daily items and pajamas and the like. Even that collection was far from tasteless.

"It's great," Yukiko uttered without thinking.

"It is, isn't it," Yoriko said with a satisfied nod.

It would do. The exhibition was elegant but also splashy.

Looking across the room, the coordinator said, "Tsukioka-san's fans are sure to be pleased." He clapped his hands and turned to look at Yukiko. "We've partitioned off the space into three rooms in the shape of a 'U' to direct the viewers through the exhibit. Your life-size figure is at the very end of the third room."

Yukiko nodded and briskly walked into the exhibition space. She followed the U-shaped path, turning right, and then right again, and there at the end stood another her. The second Yukiko, frozen in her signature dance pose and wearing her stage costume for "Flower in the Snow." It was completely identical to the woman herself.

For a moment, Yukiko thought she was looking into a mirror. When she moved her arm, she almost thought she saw the figure raising its arm to match. A chill ran up her spine as her forgotten apprehension came back to life.

As the coordinator had said, the figure was incredibly realistic, with none of a waxwork figure's typical artifice. The effect was uncanny. When she thought of the countless people who would come to gaze at her replica, she felt uncomfortable, like she was being spied upon in a private moment.

The figure seemed to radiate an aura of its creator's repulsive devotion.

Yukiko asked herself, *Can I do anything about this?* As she looked at her own smiling face, vibrant and life-like, she bit her lip in irritation. *The rest of the exhibit is fine, but maybe I can ask them just to leave this figure out of it.*

She decided that she would do exactly that. Even with that figure back in storage, the exhibit would still be able to stand on its own.

Having seen enough, she started heading back to the entrance, where her manager and the coordinator were waiting. Then, just as she was about to turn the first corner, she felt a presence behind her.

Something had stirred the air at her back.

What could that be? she wondered. She thought that she might have imagined it. Or at least, that's what she tried to make herself believe.

She sensed one thing above all: Whatever she did, she mustn't turn to look behind her. Her sixth sense warned her she would see something that could not be unseen.

Wherever that feeling came from, she didn't want to look. She couldn't look—but the more she told herself not to, the more her body rebelled against her instincts. Gradually, she began to turn to glance over her shoulder.

Before long, her upper body had turned so far around that her spine began to creak. Her eyes peered directly behind her.

Her life-size figure was still standing there—but now, something about it was even more unsettling.

Wait. What's that?

Yukiko's wide eyes opened wider. Something was entwined around her duplicate. She noticed it immediately, but in her already unsettled state, it took her mind a moment to accept what she was seeing.

The *thing* stroked her replica's face with a furry hand. Its entire body was covered with thick, fuzzy hair.

Yukiko stared in transfixed terror.

It was oddly tall. The thing teased its fingers across the figure's face, hugged its arms around the figure's chest, and lovingly caressed the figure's body.

Yukiko felt the sting of stomach juices rising up her gullet. A raw, unpleasant odor prickled at her nose; her throat made a reflexive, guttural coughing sound.

The thing's hands froze. Slowly, it turned its giant head to face Yukiko. Their eyes met.

The thing had a big, round face and two long, standing ears.

Softly, Yukiko blurted out, "It's…a rabbit?"

It was indeed a rabbit—or rather, someone in a rabbit mascot suit, a mainstay of the typical department store's rooftop play area.

Her initial reaction was almost disappointment. She felt like a fool to have felt such terror because of a rabbit. This was an event space in a department store, after all. An animal mascot was nothing out of the ordinary.

Yukiko let out a deep sigh of relief and began to observe the rabbit in more detail. The first thing she noticed was how dirty the costume was. The face, which must have once been white, was now brown with dust and grime. Its arms and legs, where they stuck out from the denim jumpsuit, were similarly filthy and knotted in patches.

I can't believe how dirty that costume is, Yukiko thought. Not long after, she wondered, *And why was it rubbing my replica all over?*

The terror began to build inside her once again and made its presence known. The right side of the rabbit's face seemed *melted*, a burn-victim mess. The eye on that side was not its cheerfully oversized self. Instead it drooped, like a piece of round candy held over an open flame.

That eye stared back at Yukiko, boring into her. The rabbit's mouth curved up in the shape of a crescent moon. Out of its center jutted two buck teeth.

"Yu…ki…ko," the rabbit said. It was a man's voice, hoarse yet strangely shrill. The combined effect was something Yukiko wished immediately to never hear again.

"Yu…ki…ko," the rabbit repeated. It pushed itself away from the figure in a slow, exaggerated motion. He took one step toward her, then another.

As if violently repelled, Yukiko turned on her heels and ran.

When Yoriko saw her come running from the exhibit space, her face pale, the manager spread her arms wide. Yukiko collapsed into her waiting arms and clung to her.

"Yukiko-chan, what's wrong?" Yoriko said. "What happened?" She took Yukiko by the shoulders and gave her a firm shake.

Yukiko's lips trembled. Her voice wavered as she muttered, "A rabbit… a rabbit…"

"What?" Yoriko shouted impatiently. "What are you talking about? What rabbit?"

Yukiko's shoulders shuddered as she pointed a weak finger toward the exhibit.

"Yukiko-chan, please get a hold of yourself! Is someone behind you? Did you see something?"

Yukiko pushed herself free from her manager and slumped down to the floor with her hands and head on her knees.

"There was," she said, pausing to gather herself, "there was a rabbit. Someone in a mascot costume. It was putting its hands all over that figure of me—that life-size figure of me."

The exhibit's coordinator was beside them, listening in. "A rabbit costume?" he said with doubt in his voice. "As far as I know, we don't have any animal costumes here."

"Are you sure it wasn't something else you saw?"

Yoriko asked. "Like he said, they don't have any animal costumes here."

Yukiko shook her head from side to side. "I'm not making this up," she said, her sentences running together. "It was really there. It was really a rabbit—and it wasn't a normal animal costume. It was dirty, and its face was burned. It was like some kind of monster. And it was coming toward me."

Yoriko looked at her face for a moment, then turned to the coordinator and said, "Well, let's go take a look. Whatever it was, she must have seen *something*." The manager put her hands on Yukiko's arms. "You stay here, Yukiko-chan. We'll go have a look. Just wait right here."

Yukiko bobbed her head once. As Yoriko and the middle-aged man disappeared down the exhibit's corridor, she thought, *What if that sinister rabbit is trying to bring some terrible disaster upon us?*

It was too late to stop her manager and the coordinator; they had already entered the exhibit. But now Yukiko worried that she had sent them into peril. With bated breath, she watched and waited for the outcome.

She didn't know how long she'd been waiting when she looked up and saw Yoriko and the coordinator in front of her. Both appeared unharmed.

Yoriko gave Yukiko a smile and said, "You can relax. No one was there. No rabbit—not even a mouse."

She turned to the coordinator and said, "Whoever it was must have run away."

"It's odd, though," the man said. "This is the only way in or out of the exhibit. The emergency exit at the rear is locked, and there's nothing else but concrete walls."

Yoriko and the man exchanged a look that seemed to say, *Maybe Yukiko was just seeing things.*

Her manager looked to her with worry. "Yukiko-chan, you've been working so hard lately."

Yukiko couldn't figure out where the rabbit had gone. Maybe Yoriko was right, and the rabbit was just some phantom conjured up in her head.

Then the idol rejected her doubt. *No. That was no trick of my mind.*

That monster had called her name. It had come after her.

That disturbing, half-melted face had been seared into her retinas—but the true source of her certainty was the distinctively repulsive and prickling smell that even now clung to the inside of her nose.

Sitting at a table in a small café near the Akasaka-mitsuke subway station, Domoto Yoriko slowly drank her cooled-off lemon tea. Across from her was a well-built gentleman in his fifties—Kanda of Kanda Projects, the talent agency to which Tsukioka Yukiko belonged.

Yoriko downed the rest of her tea and gathered her resolve before saying, "I was hoping you would consider letting Yukiko-chan take some time to rest and recuperate. I realize that this is a crucial time for her career, and she won't be able to forgo all her responsibilities, but I'd like to at least ease her schedule, even if only by a little."

"I understand where you're coming from, Yoriko-kun. But if we ease up on Yukiko's pace right now, it'll be worse for her in the long run." His voice was calm and low as he tapped his finger on the table. "I agree that Yukiko is fatigued. I also understand that you care about her like a mother cares for her child—if not more so. But right now, Yukiko needs to go full throttle, even if means having to push herself. I've been in this business for a long time now, so I know—with girls like Yukiko, everything hinges on this first sprint. So far, she's been lucky—her debut single had strong sales, and a commercial has already come in. She draws a lot of attention due to her unique position as the lone innocent-style idol persevering against the current trend. If we don't build her success into something lasting, the next thing we know, she'll be part of the past."

Yoriko nodded with each of his points, but that didn't mean she agreed with everything he said.

Kanda discovered Yukiko when she worked for a modeling agency in another part of the country, and he had gone to great lengths to get the head of that agency to give her up. It was no wonder he invested such care and enthusiasm in her. Yoriko felt the very same way.

But what Yukiko needed most now was not some future stardom. She needed rest.

Not giving up, Yoriko told Kanda everything that had happened in the department store.

Then she said, "Yukiko-chan is so exhausted, she's started to hallucinate. Please consider her situation. She's still only nineteen—just a child. She doesn't know any better. We're the adults—if we tell her to keep trying because it's for her own good, she'll listen. We'll end up forcing her to keep on pushing herself past the limits of what she can take—when what we *should* be forcing her to do is rest! Surely you must know I'm right."

She slapped her palms down on the table. The sugar pot and the cups and saucers hopped, making a tremendous clatter. The other customers turned startled stares their way.

Tears began to well in Yoriko's eyes. Kanda put his hand to his chin, then grunted and slumped in his chair.

"All right, Yoriko-kun," he said. "I'll have a talk with Yukiko. I want to hear what she has to say."

Yoriko nodded as if to say, *That'll have to do.*

Yukiko awoke with a start.

She looked to the clock beside her bed—three in the morning. Her alarm wouldn't go off for another two hours. Night sweat clung to her forehead. She must have been dreaming, though she couldn't remember it. A half-read paperback sat next to her pillow. Yukiko sat up in bed. She must have fallen asleep while reading—she thought that might have been around one in the morning, which meant she'd only slept for two hours.

I need to get back to sleep, she told herself. *Tomorrow is another hard day.*

She laid herself back down and closed her eyes. But now that she had woken up, sleep didn't return easily. After a little while, Yukiko gave up on trying to fall asleep and instead simply let herself rest. Forcing herself back to sleep would have expended more energy. Far easier for her to just rest until it was time to get up.

Yukiko stared off through the darkness at the wall across from her bed, thinking about the recent events of her life.

After her commercial aired, her former classmates—who hadn't reached out to her following her debut—got together to send her a bouquet of flowers with a card signed by all of them.

She'd received interview requests from nearly every men's weekly magazine there was.

At the planning meeting for her follow-up commercial, she met an eighty-year-old sponsor who kindly gave her a great deal of advice.

And…

And there was that other thing.

That sinister rabbit suit popped into her mind unbidden. She had tried and tried to make herself forget. Again and again, she had told herself that the rabbit was, as Yoriko said, a figment of her imagination.

After a few days, Yukiko had finally started to believe the hideous rabbit couldn't have been real. But now, in this moment, alone in her bed, the figure appeared in her mind's eye, the melted side of the rabbit's face made even more disturbing by the animal suit's former cuteness. Its short and round body was likely adorable once, but its sinister, miasma-like aura made it feel like an evil spirit.

Then there was its smell, powerful and raw, which still lingered in Yukiko's nostrils.

The singer shook her head forcefully, hoping to dispel the ever-growing vision of the rabbit from her thoughts. Whoever or whatever it was, the rabbit had vanished from the exhibit without a trace, like a puff of smoke dissipating into air.

Did that mean that, like smoke, the rabbit could go anywhere, through any crack?

The chilling thought prompted her to her feet.

With its two bedrooms, her apartment was luxuriously spacious for a woman living alone. With quick footsteps, she moved to her living room and turned on the lights, and then the TV. She pressed the play button on her VCR, which already had a tape inside it. *Edward Scissorhands*, a favorite of Yukiko's, began to play.

Portrayed by Johnny Depp in a superb performance, Edward possessed scissor blades for hands, which kept him isolated from normal humans. Yukiko was a huge fan of Depp, in no small part thanks to this film.

Her anxiety was soon soothed by the bright lights of her living room and the comfort of watching a favorite movie. Quickly, she settled into her sofa and became absorbed.

Johnny Depp tried to embrace Winona Ryder, but he couldn't complete the gesture, for fear of hurting her.

It was a rather sad scene. No matter how many times Yukiko watched it, she cried without fail. One of the nice things about living alone was being able to bawl as freely as she pleased without having to worry about anyone seeing her.

Sniffing through her runny nose, she lay down across the sofa and eventually drifted off into a peaceful slumber.

Yukiko didn't know how long she had been asleep when a sound awoke her. Through sleepy, half-lidded eyes, she saw that her living room lights had been turned off. The curtains over the sliding glass door to her balcony glowed faintly from the streetlights outside.

Just as she decided to go back to sleep, a silhouette passed across the curtains. Or at least, that's what she thought she saw. It looked like it had been a plump person with a big round stomach and a distinctively round face. From the top of its head stood two long, thin horn-like protrusions that flapped about.

It was the rabbit. It was the rabbit's shadow.

As sleep relentlessly pulled her back into its embrace, she experienced terror, pure and primal, deep down inside.

Yukiko and Yoriko sat side by side on a couch in the talent agency's reception area. Despite being managed by Kanda Projects, Yukiko had only visited this office a few times before, as her vocal and dance lessons were always held in a separate location.

She felt oddly uncomfortable here.

After a short time, Kanda Hiroshi—the agency's president—appeared around the wall of filing cabinets and metal bookcases that partitioned the reception area from the main workspace. Kanda must have been older than fifty, but his face remained smooth and shiny to an off-putting extent. He sat on a second couch facing the two women.

Yoriko greeted him without small talk. "Have you thought about what we discussed earlier?"

Kanda blinked his eyes a few times in a put-upon manner. "You mean Yukiko taking a break?" He turned to the singer. "Well, Yukiko, what do you think? Yoriko-kun has asked me to give you time to rest, but I'd like to hear your opinion."

Glancing at Yoriko, Yukiko answered, "I don't want a break. I know she'll be worried about me, and I'm sorry to do that to her, but I just want to keep doing my job."

"You don't have to do this," Yoriko pleaded. She took the singer's hand in hers. "This is a matter of your personal well-being. This goes beyond being an idol. You need to think of yourself. If you wait until you've already ruined your health, it will be too late."

Yukiko squeezed her manager's hand. "I understand," she said. "Believe me, I do. But focusing on my work is the best way to help me get through this. Taking a break sounds like the reasonable thing to do, but it actually might make things worse."

Kanda stood and said, "Then it's settled. Yukiko's schedule will go on without any changes. But for our part, we'll keep an extra close eye on her. Right, Yoriko-kun?"

Defeated, the manager rose to her feet and gave a reluctant nod. "Okay. That's what we'll do." Then to Yukiko, she said, "Your taping for *Music Standby* is today.

I'll go to the station ahead of you, but please, if at any point it gets to be too much, don't hesitate to tell us."

Yukiko grinned and said, "I'll see you there."

After Yoriko left, Kanda invited Yukiko to sit next to him, and she soon obliged. With an untroubled grin, he said, "Yoriko-kun always worries about everything. That can be a good thing, but sometimes she takes it a little too far." He winked at her as if to say, *What can you do?*

Then he added, "By the way, I have a present for you. Something came here this morning with your name on it."

Kanda reached under the table between the two facing sofas and retrieved a package. Wrapped in white paper, the box was about thirty centimeters long on either side.

"Open it and take a look," Kanda said. "I've already had a peek inside, and I have to say, it's pretty cute."

She opened the box and a rabbit tumbled out.

Yukiko gasped.

The rabbit was a wind-up figure about twenty centimeters tall. As it marched along the table, its long ears rose and fell, and it beat little drumsticks against a drum carried at its stomach.

"Well?" Kanda said, beaming. "Was I right? Cute, isn't it?"

I've had enough of that man, Yukiko thought, silently cursing her callous boss as she walked to the television station. Of all things, it had to be a toy rabbit. *How little do I matter to him?*

For days she had been tormented by visions of the rabbit. It was starting to affect her daily life. And yet Kanda had excitedly brought out that rabbit toy. He should have known that was nothing she wanted to see.

She shook her head left and right as her mind went back to that wind-up rabbit drumming away. Just remembering it gave her the chills all over again.

Subconsciously, Yukiko hurried her pace. All she could do was head to the studio where Yoriko was waiting. Her manager would understand how she was feeling.

The television station was near Akasaka's bustling commercial district—close enough to her talent agency's office to make walking her only option. She could have taken a taxi, but she didn't want to inconvenience a driver by only riding for the minimum fare. Besides, she'd been feeling like she hadn't been getting enough exercise and figured a little walk would do her good.

But even if she might have annoyed the driver, she should have taken a taxi. That, or she should have insisted that someone from the office walk with her to the TV station—for just minutes after so casually deciding to leave the office alone and on foot, she would again be confronted by blood-chilling terror.

Something's wrong, Yukiko thought.

She had just turned onto a side street near the train station. Small shops lined the narrow and sleepy street. Some were little two-story mom-and-pop operations with their residences above the street level shop and only old, weather-beaten signs to announce their presence. Others were greengrocers with fruits and vegetables left out in bins with nary a customer or proprietor in sight.

The street was so quiet that it made the bustle and noise of the nearby commercial district seem like it hadn't existed at all. Yukiko always took this street when walking to the TV station, and she recognized immediately that something was off—though she didn't know what.

Something was out of place on this familiar street. But what?

Yukiko stopped to observe.

There was the candy store that always seemed to be under the watch of the same old woman every time Yukiko passed by. Next to the store, there was a run-down cigarette stand, a greengrocer, and a shoe store.

Yukiko liked that this street was never busy. Just a few dozen meters away were teeming crowds, yet this street alone seemed left behind from another time. It offered her nostalgia and a kind of comforting loneliness. Walking past those old shops often reminded her of her hometown.

But on this day, it felt cold and unwelcoming.

Unable to locate the cause of this change, Yukiko thought, *Oh well,* and started walking again. Just a few steps later, she stopped anew. A group of excited children had gathered at the other end of the street. There were maybe ten of them, happily bouncing and laughing.

That's what's different, Yukiko realized.

Children didn't usually come to play here. When she'd turned onto this street, she must have caught a glimpse of them, and the impression they'd left on her subconscious mind had transformed the street into something unfamiliar.

That must be what's different. I'm sure of it.

Having solved the mystery, Yukiko's spirits lifted. With a sigh of relief, she walked toward the children.

They were each holding a red balloon. Someone in the middle of their circle was handing them out—probably to advertise for some nearby department store.

The sight reminded Yukiko of her own childhood. Handing out balloons on a street corner was a common way for stores to drum up business, and as a child she had received many balloons that way, much to her delight. One time, it had made her so happy that she started skipping along, and the balloon slipped from her hand and floated away into the sky.

Yukiko approached the circle of children in hopes of getting a balloon for herself, for old times' sake.

That was when the hidden figure stood up in the center of the circle.

It was a person in an animal mascot suit, nearly twice as tall as the children, and until that moment, it must have been kneeling down to hand out the balloons.

Yukiko froze.

Immediately, she closed her eyes. Something inside her told her she mustn't look.

But her eyes disobeyed. They slowly opened.

Why can't I keep my eyes closed? she asked herself, with increasing panic. *I can't look. I know it!*

Just as her eyelids were halfway open, her mind recognized what it was she was seeing.

The animal costume had a rotund body, oversized head, and two long, slender ears—it was a rabbit.

It was *the* rabbit. The source of her terror. The thing that had taught her fear like she had never known. It stood there, right before her eyes.

For a moment, she wondered if Kanda's wind-up figure had grown to ten times its size to appear here before her. The thought made her more perplexed than afraid.

But soon, her eyes opened all the way, and they stared unblinking at the rabbit. His head creaked around, fixing big round eyes on Yukiko. His right eye was distorted and drooping.

There was no room for doubt or denial. This was the same rabbit that had glided his disgusting hands up and down her life-size twin.

He seemed to recognize her. When their eyes met, the suit's ears perked up.

Keeping her eyes locked on the rabbit, Yukiko slowly backed away, careful not to make any sudden movements that might provoke him. After an excruciatingly long and frightful while, she managed to circle around the rabbit's back. Quickly, she turned and slipped out the end of the street.

She exited onto a main thoroughfare complete with its typical traffic of cars and bustling crowds. The TV station was just across the road and down a little to the right.

Yukiko patted down her chest and exhaled in relief. Yoriko was inside the station, along with the staff and crew members, many of whom were familiar to her. Once she got inside, she would be safe.

Yukiko ran up the stairs of the elevated pedestrian crossing. If she had looked over her shoulder, she would have seen something that would have made her heart leap out of her chest.

Just a few steps behind her, something followed. Whenever she went faster, it too sped up. Whenever she slowed down, it slowed down, too. Her pursuer carefully kept the distance between them the same. It seemed to be enjoying the chase.

It was, of course, the rabbit. He chased behind her, with nearly silent footsteps.

Out of breath and shoulders heaving, Yukiko reached the TV station entrance. Her fear and distress melted away, and her legs went weak. Putting force into each step, she walked up to the front doors.

She saw her reflection in the glass. Her hair was a mess, her skin blemished, and her eyes sunken. She looked like an entirely different person.

I look so old like this, she thought, with a self-deprecating smirk.

Then the little smirk froze.

Beside the exhausted woman's reflection was that of another—the rabbit.

Yukiko swallowed a startled cry.

The rabbit stood right next to her, haunting her like a ghost. His smile seemed to be directed at her frightened expression.

He followed me. He followed me this whole time, and I never even noticed.

The terror which she'd kept locked deep inside had now broken free, coursing through her body and filling her awareness. Face contorting, her swallowed-down cry came rushing back up into a wordless shriek.

She ran full speed into the TV station. So wild was her expression and so mad her charge that the front security guard couldn't even stop her. Still screaming, she fled down the lobby stairs and into the basement floor green room, where she collapsed into the arms of a puzzled-looking Yoriko.

The manager staggered back a half step but managed to catch the distraught singer.

"What's wrong?" Yoriko shouted. "Yukiko-chan! Get ahold of yourself. Get ahold of yourself!"

She slapped Yukiko on the check.

Yukiko looked at her in wide-eyed shock, and then her eyes began to fill with tears.

"Yukiko-chan," Yoriko said, "look at me. Can you calm down and tell me what happened? Please, Yukiko-chan."

Without looking away, the singer nodded her head twice. Her lips trembled, and her right cheek twitched. After an empty swallow, she forced out a tight-throated answer.

"The... the rabbit. It was the rabbit. He followed me here. He came into this building. He's still in here, somewhere. I know it."

Unable to manage any more, she covered her face with her hands.

The moment Yoriko heard the words "the rabbit," she thought, *Not this again. Another hallucination. This exhaustion is too much for her.* She felt a heartless kind of pity for the singer under her care.

As Yoriko saw it, Yukiko was still just a kid—a kid who had been plunged into the tumultuous life that came with being in the entertainment industry. Physically and mentally, the young singer had been pushed to the breaking point.

In an attempt to put Yukiko at ease, the manager walked toward the door with exaggerated movements. She threw it open.

"Here, look," Yoriko said. "There's nothing out there. There's no one in the hallway."

Fearfully, Yukiko looked at the door. Like Yoriko said, nothing was out of the ordinary.

But—*but.*

The rabbit who relentlessly pursued her was no hallucination. Yukiko was sure of that. His grimy, furry hand had been about to grab her shoulder. She hadn't dreamt or imagined that up. It had really happened.

Steeling her resolve, she walked toward Yoriko, then she pushed past the woman and into the hall.

No one was there.

"See?" Yoriko said with a bright smile. "Nothing."

Not quite able to accept it, Yukiko shook her head and said, "But…"

Yoriko spoke soothingly. "In any case, that scary rabbit is gone. You don't have to worry anymore."

She's right, Yukiko thought as her nerves slowly settled. *The rabbit is gone. I don't need to be afraid.*

She felt her heart begin to slow, and her shoulders grew heavy. She sat down in a chair at a makeup table and let out a deep sigh, then absently gazed off at a ceiling-mounted TV playing a relay feed from a studio camera upstairs.

Yoriko put her arm around her and spoke softly into her ear. "Yukiko-chan," she said, "once you get through this appearance today, take a little break, okay? You must be exhausted. And you know what—I am, too. A little rest would do us both some good."

Yukiko took her manager's hand and squeezed it tight. "Thank you. Your concern means a lot to me, and it's great that you're looking out for me. But I'm fine. I'm not exhausted. It's that rabbit that's upsetting me, nothing else."

Yoriko wanted to say, *Those hallucinations are proof of your exhaustion.* But she sensed that saying that would only serve to put more strain on the girl's already fragile mind, so she kept it to herself.

Yoriko squeezed Yukiko's hand back and gave the singer a *there, there* pat on the shoulder.

Yukiko leaned back in the chair and looked at the vanity mirror. Her sunken-eyed face was reflected back at her.

I do look tired, she admitted to herself. *Yoriko is right.*

Her lips formed a wry smile as she thought of how her manager knew her own body better than herself.

She really is incredible, Yukiko thought. She turned her head to look to Yoriko.

The two women's eyes met. They nodded to each other without breaking their gaze.

Yoriko-san worries about me like I were her own sister, and I trust in her, from the bottom of my heart.

Yukiko suddenly wanted to hug the woman. In this city of strangers, Yoriko was the only person who felt like family. Fat tears began to drip from the singer's eyes and blurred her vision so that she could no longer see the image on the ceiling-mounted monitor.

"I can't believe I'm crying like this," Yukiko said, wiping away her tears. "What's gotten into me?"

On the monitor, various crew members were constructing the set for the eight o'clock live broadcast music show. Yukiko had been on the show a few times now, and she always liked to get an advance look at the set through the makeup room's monitor. That way, she could decide which outfit would best match the set's design and color.

Yoriko looked up at the TV screen and said, "No matter how many times I see the sets they build for *Music Standby*, it's always dazzling."

Yukiko nodded. "If there were more shows like this one," she said, "it would go a long way toward lifting up the idol business."

The two women watched the bustling crew with some measure of hope in their eyes.

"Huh?" Yoriko said as the monitor went black.

Someone seemed to have moved directly in front of the camera—probably some oafish crewmember casually standing there, not realizing that anyone might be watching the feed. But soon it became evident that that someone wasn't just standing there by chance. They were doing it on purpose.

And then the person moved, leaning face-first into the lens.

Yukiko felt the hairs over her body stand on end. Something inside her told her to look away from the screen before she saw anything else. *It's the rabbit,* she told herself. *It has to be the rabbit. I mustn't look, no matter what.*

But, defying her will, her eyes remained fixed on the screen.

The face came right up to the lens like someone playing peekaboo. And, as she had dreaded, the face was not that of a human.

It was round and furry.

It had two big, wide-open eyes.

It had an upturned mouth.

It had two buck teeth.

It had two long, skinny ears.

It was the rabbit. It was that damned rabbit mascot.

Yoriko let out a little gasp.

Yukiko's eyes widened as big as they could.

The rabbit's mouth grinned even wider. It let out an eerie laugh that could have easily come from a witch or some ghostly monster.

One of its eyes had sagged from its socket. Small patches of fur were burned away here and there along its arms.

Yoriko thought, *This is it. This is the monster Yukiko was talking about—real, not imagined. This is Yukiko's tormentor.*

Yoriko shouted, "Someone, anyone, come here!"

As Yukiko heard her manager shout for help, she felt her consciousness slipping away.

With a bitter shake of his head, Kanda grumbled, "I spoke with an acquaintance of mine on the police force.

Like I feared, the detective said it just wasn't enough for them to do anything."

Her temper flaring, Yoriko said, "But look at how she's been hurt. Is causing mental anguish not a crime?"

The agency's president shook his head again. "It's not. I think you're right—mental and emotional pain is every bit as serious as physical pain. But unless that rabbit bastard inflicts tangible, physical harm, the police won't act. That's just the way it is. Frightening someone isn't even a misdemeanor."

"Then what can we do? If we wait until something has already happened, it'll be too late. Shouldn't the police be interested in preventing crime from happening in the first place? If they won't do anything, we have to think of what *we* can do—otherwise Yukiko won't be able to feel safe anywhere."

The image of that rabbit's menacing face on the studio feed would likely remain with her forever. Only when she saw it did she understand Yukiko's terror. It was no wonder the singer had been so out of sorts lately.

That rabbit had waltzed right into the TV station and disappeared without a trace. The same had happened at the department store. Only minutes after Yukiko saw the rabbit, he had vanished.

After arriving in response to Yoriko's shouts for help, a group of the TV station's employees searched all around the studio. But they found neither hide nor grimy hair of the rabbit. This wasn't just someone in an animal suit. He was capable of misdirection and deception to an almost supernatural degree.

Yoriko said, "What we need to do—the only thing we can and must do—is form our own protective squad."

"Don't you think that's going a little too far?" Kanda asked. He hadn't seen the rabbit with his own eyes. He didn't even begin to try to understand Yoriko and Yukiko's fear. As far as he was concerned, they were being a bit hysterical.

"No, it's not going too far," Yoriko said, "and I'm doing it with or without your approval. In fact, I've already decided who will form the squad."

"You have?" Kanda asked.

"That's right. And I expected you might not be on board with my plan, so I took the liberty of getting started on my own." She turned to the door and said, "Yuji-kun, you can come in now."

The door slowly opened, and a boy hesitantly walked in. With his long hair and sharp-eyed expression, he tried to make himself look like an adult, but more likely than not he was just barely high school age.

He bowed his head to Kanda.

"You probably know him already," Yoriko said to Kanda. "This is Oe Yuji, the president of Yukiko's fan club—the Snow Children."

Kanda hadn't recognized the boy at first, but the introduction jolted his memory. They had met once before, right after Yukiko's debut when the nascent fan club's president came to this office.

Yoriko continued, saying, "I'm sure you're aware of how much he's done for us. He arranges for the club members to come to Yukiko's events as a group, helps promote her campaigns, and much more."

"Certainly, I am," Kanda said. "And I'm very grateful for it."

He glanced at Yuji, who bashfully lowered his head to look away.

Yoriko said, "I know it's asking a lot of the club, but I know they want to help, and I think we should let them. Isn't that right, Yuji-kun?"

The boy stood at attention, puffed out his chest, and said, "Leave it to us, Yoriko-san. We're ready to give our lives to protect Yukiko-san."

Kanda was taken a little aback by the kid's militaristic eagerness to serve, but he also recognized that it was the perfect attitude for an ad hoc bodyguard.

"All right," Kanda said, "we'll do it Yoriko-kun's way." He looked to the kid and said, "We'll be counting on you."

Yuji bobbed his head deeply. "Thank you, sir. I will

see to Yukiko-san's absolute safety. I'll convey the orders to my subordinates immediately."

Shimizu Kunio walked down the poorly-lit street, savoring a certain sense of fulfillment.

A chic apartment building was visible in the gaps between the branches of the carefully maintained row of bushes alongside the street. When Kunio thought of how Tsukioka Yukiko was somewhere in that building, he felt pleasure spring up from deep in his chest. The sensation was powerful enough to make him tremble.

I'm so glad I joined the fan club, Kunio thought fervently. His passionate support for Yukiko had been rewarded.

If he hadn't joined her fan club and been active in the inner circle, he would have never ended up here, standing outside her apartment, let alone with the honor of being her protector.

Kunio glanced at his wristwatch. It was two in the morning. Yukiko was probably asleep by now.

Kunio imagined the idol wearing pajamas with some cute pattern on them, breathing softly and adorably in her sleep. He remained vigilant to ensure that she could remain slumbering peacefully until daylight came.

Kunio had joined Yukiko's fan club almost half a year ago, and he always cheered loudly for her at her events.

His passionate support caught the attention of the fan club's management (specifically, the head of the inner circle, Oe Yuji), who invited him into the elite group of Yukiko's most ardent fans.

Being in the inner circle was not easy, and the privilege came with rigid rules and severe expectations. They had to clear their lives to match Tsukioka Yukiko's schedule. The moment he was in, he was no longer his own person.

Yuji had told him, "Tsukioka Yukiko-san is a treasure—one that we must protect even if it means risking our own lives. We must do everything within our power to support Yukiko-san so that she can become an even bigger star. You must understand that when you join us, you lose your personal freedom."

Kunio nodded deeply in response. He felt his back muscles tense up.

After graduating high school, he found a job at a nearby factory, but it didn't fulfill him. He felt like he was just going through the motions of life.

The moment he saw Yukiko on TV, everything changed. For the first time, he felt complete. The transformation in his life was like a monochrome screen coming into full color.

His tedious job at the factory became easy when he thought of it as something he did for her. He was willing to give her everything—that was how valuable she was to him. Nearly every moment not spent at work was spent on supporting Yukiko and cheering her on. Without fail, he bought every new CD and photo book on the release date—not a day later. Whenever she had a local event or performance, nothing could prevent him from going to see her.

Why was he drawn to her with such intensity? Probably because she came off as sharing some of his negative qualities—in particular, timidity and introversion. Whatever the underlying reasons, his passion as a fan brought him into her fan club, got him invited into the inner circle, and now found him standing on guard outside her apartment.

Even within that inner circle, the hierarchy was firmly established, and good conduct was a must. As with such groups, simply being a member of the elite did not mean a fan would get any closer to the subject of their cause. In fact, they had to remain at a greater distance than the typical fan.

The very top management got to be on familiar conversational terms with her, but to new recruits like Kunio, even speaking to her would be like a dream within a dream.

But now here he was, keeping watch over her through the night. How could a fan be more blessed than that?

Kunio didn't know *why* he was keeping watch. He hadn't even the slightest idea. Yuji's orders were to guard the area around Yukiko's apartment building until morning. That was it. It wouldn't have been in Kunio's place to ask any questions, nor did he even entertain the thought.

He was happy to simply be near Yukiko, no matter what the circumstances might have been.

All that I must do, he thought, *is stay on the alert so that Yukiko-san can sleep without worry.* Even as his thoughts got carried away, romanticizing his role as her protector, his sense of duty burned inside him like an open flame. He kept a sharp eye on the darkened streets.

Maybe some deranged, malicious fan is stalking her around her neighborhood. My mission might be to protect her from him.

Kunio wondered what he would be like if he were that kind of fan instead. Wouldn't he be around here somewhere, stalking her around her neighborhood, hoping to accomplish some sinister goal?

I won't let him!

Even as he thought this, another part of him wrestled with the possibility that some twist of fate could have turned him into the very person he was out to stop.

And so, as he carried out his commander's orders, and though he was fired up by his duty to protect Yukiko, his conflicting emotions swirled about inside him with no signs of stopping.

A rustle came from the bushes.

Someone was hiding in the shadows.

From what Kunio could see, the lurking figure was crouched over, completely still. The intruder appeared to be trying to get a look inside the apartments.

Kunio thought, *Is this the bastard who's stalking Yukiko-chan?* Then, without any hesitation, he resolved himself. *I'm going to chase him away!*

On silent footsteps, Kunio approached the suspicious figure. He got a better angle through the bushes and saw that someone was indeed crouched there.

This wasn't a normal person. He was gigantic. For a moment, Kunio's resolve wavered, and he gulped down a breath of air.

The intruder must have sensed someone was near, because he swiftly arose. He had a furry body, denim overalls, and a round face twice as large as a man's.

What? Kunio thought, feeling almost disappointed. *It's someone in a rabbit costume.*

What potential threat did a person in a rabbit suit pose to Yukiko? Kunio had only known mascot characters to hand out balloons to kids, or flyers to passersby. They were friends to children.

Kunio was puzzled. He asked himself, *What is some-one in a rabbit costume doing here? Shouldn't he be in some department store's rooftop amusement park? And it's the middle of the night, too.*

Suddenly, the rabbit turned toward Kunio.

It was then that he saw the face. What he had assumed would be the lovable visage of a cartoon rabbit was instead a half-melted, monstrous thing.

Kunio held down a scream.

The rabbit's ears stood up.

The would-be bodyguard understood instinctively what that meant—the rabbit was going to attack.

Kunio took one step back, and then another.

The rabbit swayed his way through a gap in the bushes, and then emerged.

Kunio's legs froze as he looked up at the giant rabbit. *I-I have to run. I have to run now.*

That's what he told himself, but his body refused to listen. His only movement was the fearful shaking in his face. For the first time in his life, Kunio knew true terror.

Slowly, the rabbit walked forward, stopping right in front of the young man. A piercing, repulsive smell came drifting from the suit.

In a hoarse, inhuman voice, the rabbit said, "You're shaking."

Kunio thought he glimpsed two evil eyes staring out

at him from the rabbit's mouth.

The rabbit raised a furry hand and grabbed Kunio by the shoulder. The hand felt soft and rubbery. In that instant, Kunio's body came back into motion. He rocked his shoulder, pushing away the rabbit's hand, and with a wordless battle cry, he threw himself at the creature.

Kunio's terror powered him, and he found himself filled with a strength he had never known he possessed.

The rabbit fell over backward into the bushes, and Kunio went with him. The young man sat up, straddling the rabbit, and put his hands around the suit's fat neck. On the other side of the scratchy fabric, he felt an unexpectedly slender human neck. All he had to do was squeeze. He put all his strength into the task, strangling the rabbit as hard as he could.

The rabbit flailed his arms and legs. Sweat rolled down Kunio's forehead as he kept on squeezing.

Just then, the rabbit's cutesy mouth curled into a twisted snarl, and a voice rasped out. "I'll...kill...you." The scratchy voice, muffled by the mask, sent an even deeper terror into Kunio. "I'm running out of time—not that you'd understand. September twenty-sixth. Her first live stage performance will be on the Marusho roof."

Kunio fought the rising urge to run away screaming and instead put everything he had into squeezing the rabbit's neck. The creature swung up his arm and drove an open palm strike into Kunio's face from below.

Kunio's head rocked back. His arms weakened. Then the rabbit was back on his feet, grabbing the stunned Kunio by both shoulders. He plunged his giant head toward the young man's face.

Again and again, the rabbit head-butted him. The costume's head was only a shell constructed out of light materials, but after enough strikes Kunio's face began to welt and bleed.

Kunio no longer had any fight left in him, but the crazed rabbit kept slamming his head into the young man's face. At some point, Kunio lost consciousness. His upper body had gone limp, and he rocked back and forth like a wooden marionette, each forward motion met with another strike. His face was a disfigured mess. Wide rivers of red blood flowed freely from his eyes, his nose, his mouth, and from wherever the skin had rent with another opening. An occasional gasping cough indicated he was still alive.

The rabbit took Kunio's bloody face in both hands and pulled it up against his own. Then he whispered, "I'll do this to anyone who tries to get in between me and Yukiko. And don't you forget it."

Yukiko sat at a makeup table in the green room provided for her by the Marusho department store staff. As she applied her makeup, she thought about her decision to go forward with the concert.

She was scared, certainly. She was very scared.

She knew she should have begged and pleaded to call off the event, but she'd done nothing of the sort.

It was the last thing she wanted to do, really—even after her manager gave her an easy way out, saying, "If you don't want to do this, you don't have to. I can come up with an excuse for you."

It was a nice offer, but Yukiko viewed canceling her performance as letting that repugnant rabbit win. She didn't want to lose—especially not to that rabbit. Her hatred toward her costumed stalker had grown into something too large for her to keep in check. What better revenge could she have than capping off her successful exhibit with a stellar live performance?

The police hadn't been able to find Shimizu Kunio, a volunteer bodyguard who had gone missing from outside her apartment. Only the police and the young man's direct relatives knew of his disappearance. The president of Yukiko's fan club had gone to great lengths to ensure that the media remained ignorant of her volunteer security force.

Had the media found out about Kunio's disappearance, reporters would have been on her like a pack of hyenas. Blaming her would have made for a great scandal.

Yukiko worried that the rabbit might have done something to the man, though she kept the thought to herself. She didn't even tell Yoriko.

The rabbit's true intentions remained a total unknown. All Yukiko knew was that he seemed to be fixated on her. Perhaps his ultimate goal was to make Yukiko his. If that were the case, then it stood to reason that he had attacked Kunio for interfering. Yukiko was convinced that logic was sound.

Up until now, the rabbit had terrorized Yukiko by appearing near her. But that was all he had done. He struck terror into her only to vanish like so much mist. That was his consistent pattern.

But now he had attacked someone. Even if that person had interfered, the change in the rabbit's behavior was alarming. Had he finally revealed his true, violent nature?

She didn't think that was what had happened—or at least, not exactly. Instead, she believed that the rabbit was now prepared to get her by any means necessary.

Yukiko shivered. Apparently, she hadn't fully numbed herself to the terror.

Will he come here? she asked herself, then answered, *He will. I'm sure of it.*

But she wasn't going to let him do as he pleased any longer. She was going to hold her concert just as planned, and if the rabbit came, she wouldn't be alone. The talent agency's staff was on hand, along with Oe Yuji—hungry to avenge his comrade—and a group of plainclothes cops there on Kanda's insistence. Surely, they would be able to subdue him.

Yukiko glanced over to Yoriko, who was sitting on a sofa near the makeup table. Her manager looked on with a troubled brow.

The singer gave her as bright a smile as she could muster and said, "Yoriko-san, try not to think about it too much. If he comes, he comes."

Yoriko nodded in acceptance. "Well, put on a good show today," the manager said, sounding more reassuring than Yukiko could have managed in her position. "I took a peek at the audience, and the seats are absolutely packed. I heard there are hundreds who couldn't even get in."

"I'm glad to hear it," Yukiko said without pausing at her makeup. "Sometimes it's easy to forget how grateful I am to have them." She reached for the outfit she'd chosen for the event, then asked, "How much longer until I go on?"

Yoriko glanced at her watch. "About fifteen minutes."

Nearly half of the Marusho department store's rooftop space had been reserved for the live concert. The ice cream, yakisoba, and various other food stands had been cleared away, and a stage erected in front of the open space.

These department store temporary event spaces were often slapdash affairs, but Marusho went to the effort of doing it right. The stage platform scaffolding was solidly in place, and they had even set up a stage truss complete with lights.

Some four hundred chairs had been provided, and all of them were full. A standing-room crowd made up another three hundred or so attendees. People had even filled the rooftop's amusement area, where there was a modest carousel, single-seat miniature trains, and other smaller-scale attractions. According to the event organizer, Marusho had never had a more highly-attended event.

As Yukiko walked from the green room to the back-stage wing, she looked out at the packed crowd and couldn't help but feel deeply moved.

There's so many people, she thought. *And they're all here to support me.*

Yukiko hadn't become an idol because she wanted to be one. The talent agency had decided that was what she was going to do. It wasn't an idea that had come from within her. "Pop idol" was simply a role for her to fill. But as her fans' outpouring of excited kinetic energy washed over her, for the first time, she felt glad she had become an idol. Now it was her turn to repay them by putting on the very best show she could. She focused her mind on the show, and determination filled her completely.

As long as she was an idol, she would always have followers who weren't normal. Unbalanced fans would be drawn to her—and perverts, too. Some might try to threaten her like the man in the rabbit suit.

Yukiko drew strength from the cheering crowd and redoubled her resolve. *I refuse to let them beat me!*

A single plainclothes policeman stood at his post next to the freight elevator at the rear of the event hall holding Yukiko's exhibit. His job was to check every person who went in or out of that elevator.

But he hadn't been given any concrete details from his superiors—he was only told to watch for "suspicious-looking individuals."

He knew that a popular idol singer named Tsukioka Yukiko was making an appearance up on the roof, but as far as he knew, he wasn't there for her protection. His best guess was that he had been posted in case there was a stampede and mass panic.

This is an awful lot of fuss for just one girl, he thought. He was supposed to have had the day off and wasn't especially happy about being forced to work an overtime shift instead.

The policeman had seen Tsukioka Yukiko sing on television once. She looked mild-mannered and mostly unremarkable, and he remembered her voice as being nothing special, either. So why on earth were so many people coming to see such an ordinary girl?

The world is full of things that don't make any sense, thought the officer, who was atypically closed-minded for a man only in his mid-twenties.

That was when it happened.

The freight elevator's rusty metal doors groaned open with a terrible scraping sound. For a moment, the policeman's body went rigid. From the first moment he saw the figure that stepped out from the elevator, he thought he sensed a malicious presence—something too horrifying to be witnessed by the human eye. But what emerged was nothing but an adorable animal mascot—a rabbit in overalls. Its ears stood straight up.

It's just someone in a costume, he thought in a mixture of relief and anticlimactic disappointment. The rabbit was probably part of the rooftop amusement park.

The policeman let out a deep sigh. When he was in college, he took a job as a mascot for just a single day. He had been a rabbit, too. It had been a sweltering day in the middle of summer break, and the inside of the costume had been hotter than hell. Just one hour wearing it put him in a state of dehydration.

With the wistful remembrance of a hardship passed, the policeman watched the rabbit walk by. It gave him a slight bow and walked toward the emergency staircase that lead up to the back end of the roof.

Noticing that patches of the rabbit's fur were knotted up, the policeman muttered, "Someone oughta clean that thing."

He must be headed up to the roof to give out balloons to the kids, he thought.

But something still bothered him. Why had he felt that momentary terror at seeing the rabbit? As he tilted his head in bewilderment, he kept his eyes on the door to the staircase where the rabbit had gone.

With a deeply concerned expression, Yoriko said, "It's not too late. Can't we still call this off somehow?"

"Yoriko-kun," Kanda said with a not-this-again scowl, "why do you always have to be like this? You know we can't cancel the show now. You've been in this business long enough to understand full well what would happen if we did. Besides, Yukiko is standing by, ready to go, and in good spirits."

Kanda and Yoriko were seated in the small rooftop level office Yukiko was using for a green room. From the window, they could see the singer standing in the stage wing, waiting for her cue.

"Of course, I know what would happen," Yoriko said, "but I still say we need to cancel it. Call it a woman's intuition. I can't shake the feeling that something terrible is about to happen."

Kanda let out a heavy sigh and pressed his palms against his knees. "Let me guess—that phantom rabbit will appear again. And he'll attack Yukiko like he did Shimizu-kun."

"I don't appreciate you making light of this," Yoriko said. "I'm serious. I'm deeply worried about what could happen to Yukiko-chan."

Kanda put his hand on her shoulder. "Listen. I understand how you feel. I wasn't joking. I really do think that rabbit got Shimizu-kun. That's why I convinced my police chief friend to give us three plainclothes officers for the day. Yukiko's volunteer guards are operating in groups of two, and I've assigned them posts throughout the event space. The department store's security and staff are on alert, ready to act the moment anything happens. Even if that rabbit does show up, he won't be able to lay a finger on Yukiko."

Yoriko felt somewhat reassured by his words, but her expression remained unconvinced. "I am worried about that rabbit," she said, "but that's not all I'm afraid of. What really concerns me are all those people."

She turned her eyes to the sea of Yukiko's fans that

filled the roof.

"What are you talking about?" Kanda said with surprise. "We should be glad they're here. No idol inspires this much excitement these days. We need to nurture that kind of audience, not fear them."

Yoriko's face remained grim. "There could be a panic."

"A panic?"

"That's right," Yoriko said. "Think about it. The roof is packed to the brim. If there are police officers here, they sure aren't enforcing the fire code for capacity." As she spoke, she became more and more agitated. "The crowd stretches all the way down the staircase. And they're all here with one single-minded purpose—to see Yukiko-chan. Even the smallest accident could turn into a catastrophe."

Her bleak tone unsettled Kanda, but he said, "You're overthinking things, Yoriko-kun. Anyway, the show will start in a matter of minutes, and it'll all be over within an hour. Can't we just cheer up a little for her big moment?"

In the stage's wing, Yukiko was checking over her outfit one last time. She had on a white turtleneck sweater over a black corduroy dress. The dress went down to just above her knees, revealing athletic legs clad in black stockings. For her shoes, she had gone with her favorite pair of black pumps.

She put her hands together and said a little prayer

to herself. It was something she always did before every event, be it a TV appearance or a handshake meet-and-greet.

The busy backstage staff all looked nervous for the performance. The PA engineer finished readying the tape containing Yukiko's backing tracks as he listened to orders coming over his headset.

It was about to start.

The fans' cheers swelled like a tidal wave. Hollers and whistles and foot stomps resounded across the roof. This was to be Yukiko's first real live performance, and as she felt the crowd's anticipation, her legs began to shake.

"God, please look over me," she said under her breath. "Please allow this event to be a success." Then, fired up, she turned toward the stage.

The audience's shouts began to sound almost furious. Their anticipation to see Tsukioka Yukiko live was driving them wilder and wilder.

At the entrance to the rooftop, a security guard was arguing with the line of fans. The crowd was attempting to press through the entrance and tempers had flared.

"It's free admission," a long-haired youth at the front of the pack said. "There're no tickets! So let me in already."

He pushed against the security guard's chest and

tried to get by. The guard quickly pushed the young man back. As they struggled, the angry fan grunted and growled, and a group of other fans pushed at his back.

The guard reached for the transceiver radio at his belt so that he could call for backup. But before he could, a high-pitched man's voice came from somewhere down the stairs. The rooftop was a cacophony of crowd noises, but somehow the shrill voice pierced through the din and across the audience.

"It's Tsukioka Yukiko!"

The first to react was the long-haired youth trying to force his way past the guard. He shouted, "She's—she's down there?" and turned and ran down the stairs.

That was the spark. All the fans who hadn't made it onto the rooftop ran down the stairs after him. They knocked down a child playing on the landing where the stairs doubled back. The boy began to scream and cry, but the child's voice only agitated the crowd and spurred them to run faster.

It wasn't just the fans at the rooftop's entrance now, either. The entire audience stood up from their seats.

"It looks like Yukiko-chan isn't appearing on stage, but down in the exhibit," said one.

"She's not coming here?" cried another.

"Behind us," a third shouted. "Behind us! Yukiko is back that way!"

Standing at the seat he'd secured in the front row, one impassioned fan looked to be in shock. His face went pale. Then he was scrambling to pack away his tripod-mounted camera, and made a dash for the staircase, attempting to beat the rest of the crowd to the punch.

Folding chairs began to tumble over. Attendees started getting swept away and knocked down by the surging crowd. Angry shouts arose all around. One simple phrase shouted by one heartless person had thrown the entire area into total panic.

Kanda and Yoriko burst out from the green room. For a brief second, they both froze in shock at the erupting chaos, then quickly regained composure and began shouting orders to the security team and staff.

For a moment, Yukiko didn't realize what was going on. One minute, she was ready to step on stage and deliver her best performance, and the next, angry shouts filled the air, and her fans all stood up at once.

Hundreds of people took off running at the same time and in the same direction like a herd of stampeding buffalo. Yukiko watched the stampede aghast, but for some reason, her emotions remained utterly calm. At one point, she thought, *This is like that scene from* The Lion King.

Not knowing what she should do, the idol returned to the green room to look for Yoriko. The event would likely be canceled. The stampede might not go without injuries. If that happened, those hyena-like newspaper reporters would come around looking for someone to blame. For that reason—and every other—she hoped that no one would be hurt.

When she reached the green room, no one was inside. She considered returning to the stage, but thought better of it and instead decided to leave via the emergency staircase down the hall from the green room. If anyone saw her back on stage, the chaos would only increase. For now, she would go to the staff room next to her exhibit.

Hurrying now, she exited the green room and turned right. Stacks of cardboard boxes lined the hall, narrowing the passage there. Beyond the boxes, a metal fire door led to the stairs.

The hallway's fluorescent lights didn't quite reach to the end of the hall. The dimly lit space made Yukiko feel nervous.

Under her breath, she told herself, "I need to find Yoriko-san as fast as I can." Walking quickly, she headed for the end of the hall.

Then, just as she slipped past the stacks of boxes, she heard a rustling noise behind her. Reflexively, she looked over her shoulder. Farther down the hall, a figure stood backlit by the soft glow coming from the green room. For a moment, Yukiko's mind froze.

Then she wished it had stayed that way. She recognized who it was easily—it was the last person she wanted to meet.

It was the rabbit—that monster. Until now, he had been lurking around her like a shadow, but now he had come to confront her directly.

The event area had descended into chaos, stretching the heavy security thin. The rabbit hadn't failed to capitalize on the opportunity. He'd waited for the security to go out onto the roof, and when they were all outside, he went inside.

He's worked through every detail, Yukiko thought. Keeping her eyes on him, she slowly backed away.

Silhouetted by the lights, the rabbit's ears stood up. He had seen her.

An indistinct growl came from his mouth. Was he enraged or elated? Yukiko couldn't tell. Whatever the case, the rabbit was excited.

Overwhelming terror hit her in waves, so strong they might have made her faint. But deep down, she remained surprisingly calm.

Maybe I'm more resilient than I look, she thought.

In a dark hallway, she faced down this rabbit, whose true identity and capabilities remained a mystery. If this wasn't danger, then nothing was. And yet she stood against him in full control of her emotions. Perhaps facing him out in the open and so close up had enabled her newfound resolve.

As she backed away, she reached her hand behind her in search of the fire door's handle. The rabbit tilted his head quizzically. He seemed to be trying to figure out what she was doing.

Her fingers touched cold metal. *The fire door,* she thought. Her hand quickly found the handle and turned it without a moment's pause.

The door clicked open.

Hearing the sound, the rabbit shook his head. Letting out an unnatural scream, he sprang into a charging run.

As soon as she had slipped through the open door, she flung it shut. As the door swung closed, the rabbit barreled straight into it. The metal shook, and the impact sent Yukiko flying backward.

The rabbit rebounded, landing in a heap just on the other side. It looked as if he'd been at least mildly concussed.

Yukiko landed hard on her backside. She had to struggle to breathe through the sharp pain, but she managed to scramble to her feet and flee down the stairway.

The rabbit held his hands to his head and arose unsteadily.

Yukiko came running into the staff room shouting unintelligibly. But the dreary, bare concrete room was empty. Everyone had gone up to the roof.

Yukiko's shoulders slumped in disappointment. The rabbit was still pursuing her, but no one was here to come to her rescue. She turned around to face the door she'd left half-open behind her, and the rabbit suddenly appeared in the gap.

Yukiko jumped and let out a startled peep, then quickly looked around for anything she could use to defend herself.

On the table in the center of the room was a large and heavy glass ashtray. She grabbed it and faced the rabbit, weapon at the ready. The rabbit chuckled. His big, round left eye blinked at her, as did the half-melted right one, its eyelid twitching erratically up and down. It was an utterly repulsive sight.

Yukiko rushed at the rabbit, taking the ashtray in both hands and swinging it hard against the rabbit's fat head. A startled, muffled grunt emanated from inside the costume, and the rabbit sank down to the floor. Again Yukiko beat the ashtray against the top of the rabbit's head, and then again and again. She kept on striking him, not even stopping when her arms began to tire and her muscles began to ache.

The costume's forehead split open, revealing a cottonlike backing. It looked like the rabbit's gray matter was spilling out, and the sight was oddly chilling.

The rabbit glared up at her and curled up the corners of its buck-toothed mouth into a ghastly smile. Yukiko's hands froze for a fraction of an instant.

That was all the time the rabbit needed to reach up with his furry hands and grab her around her slender waist. He yanked her down against him. Yukiko flailed with her entire body, but the rabbit's strength overpowered her, and he drew her into a bear hug.

The idol's arms were still free. She pushed against his sides and his stomach to try to escape, but he held her firm. The rabbit's face, sinister and unnerving, was right up next to hers. At such a close range, it seemed absurdly huge. She could see each and every hair, and the melted plastic eye bulged out in gruesome close-up detail, while the foul smell of ammonia and sweat radiated from inside the suit and assaulted her nostrils.

Lifting her in his arms, the rabbit walked to the rear of the staff room and dumped her onto the linoleum floor. The cold tiles pressed into her back.

I have to escape, she thought, pushing herself up from the floor, but the rabbit pinned her in place. The suit's stench was overwhelming and nearly gagged her.

The rabbit lay down beside Yukiko, as if they were cuddling. He pulled her against his chest. Her eyes were now level with the rabbit's mouth. In the back of that gaping maw, two small points glistened. She looked at those points—not with any purpose, but because there was nowhere else for her to look. Her eyesight wasn't perfect, and at first, she couldn't tell what she was seeing. Then, after a moment, she thought she might know what they were.

They were the eyes of the man inside the costume. That had to be it. They were the eyes of the unknown man who had relentlessly stalked and tormented her. They were staring at her with ominous excitement.

Yukiko saw the obsession in those eyes, and it gave her goosebumps.

The rabbit tightened his arm around her, and with his free hand—an oversized, soft hand—he caressed her long hair.

"Yu...ki...ko..."

His hoarse voice stabbed into her ears. Sticky breath fell across her face. As if that weren't unsettling enough, the rabbit pressed his giant face against hers, and a warm, sluglike thing popped out from its mouth.

Then, it licked across her face.

It was his tongue, wet and slimy, but also with an animal's rough, sandpapery texture. The urge to vomit filled her chest, and she pushed at the rabbit's face with both hands.

"Stop it!" she shouted. "Please, stop!"

The rabbit redoubled the strength of his grasp. With his scratchy voice, he coaxed her, "Yukiko... I love you. I don't want anyone else to have you."

Even without all that was happening to her, the freak's confession of love would have been enough to repulse her to her core.

The rabbit's hand began feeling at her chest, squeezing her smallish breasts like he knew what he was doing. He let out a deep breath in ecstasy, and his fingers moved down between her legs. Yukiko's body began to tremble, but certainly not from pleasure. The sheer horror of it all sent shivers cascading through her nervous system.

Desperately seeking to escape from this hell, Yukiko flailed her arms and legs. But the rabbit's oversized body was all around her, and it would have taken a lot more than that to break free.

The rabbit hugged his arms around her and slithered his tongue across her face. "I love you so much," he whispered with his foul breath. "So, so much."

Yukiko managed to wrestle her right arm free. "I don't want to be loved by someone like you!" she shouted.

She jabbed her hand into the rabbit's gaping, grinning mouth. Her fingers made contact with something squishy—the eyes of the man inside the suit, she thought. She was quickly proved right as the man's unrelentingly powerful arms slackened, and a muffled grunt escaped the rabbit's head.

Yukiko shoved away his weakened arms and kicked at him as hard as she could with both feet. Her skirt fluttered up distastefully, but she had no time to worry about appearances.

The rabbit rolled about on the floor holding his arms to his mouth. She watched him for a moment then snapped out of it and left the room. When she reached the landing to the stairs, she faced a choice. Go up to the roof or down to the lower floors. She hesitated for a moment. Then, thinking that the panic might have settled down by now, she chose the roof. As she started climbing the stairs, she heard a doleful voice coming from behind her.

"Yu…ki…ko."

She looked, and the rabbit was there, blindly swinging his arms about as he came toward her. He seemed to be having a great deal of trouble seeing after her eye jab. Watching him stagger and wind toward her, she froze for a second but quickly recovered and fled up the stairs.

As she stood at the doorway leading to the rooftop, the rabbit crawled up the stairs after her, slowly and steadily, moving like a lizard on his hands and feet.

Yukiko flung open the door and found a small, separate rooftop occupied by a water tower and a fenced-in power transformer unit. Her heart sank. Where *was* she? She must have taken a wrong turn and now she was cornered.

The rabbit was still coming after her. If she didn't quickly find a way to escape, he'd capture her again. But there was nowhere to run.

She turned and watched him coming up the stairs. She must have really hurt his eyes, because he appeared to be climbing each step with great effort.

She wondered if she could jump over him and run back downstairs. Yet injured eyes or not, he still possessed overwhelming strength. If he managed to catch her again, it would likely mean her life.

She slipped around the side of the water tower and stood beside the chain-link fence. A metal sign affixed to the fence read DANGER: HIGH VOLTAGE CURRENT. The idol started to climb over the fence, but the sign gave her a moment's pause.

That pause was her ruin.

The rabbit had managed to catch up to her. He put his hand on the back of her head and twisted it toward him until her eyes were on his ugly face. A lazy trail of blood dangled from the rabbit's mouth. She must have scratched his eyes.

His shoulders rising and falling with each breath, the rabbit said, "That was cruel, Yukiko. Why would you hurt me like that? Can't you see how much I love you? How could you be so mean to me?"

He rattled her head, and then again, and then once more.

His voice went eerily quiet. "I could just keep turning your head around."

His fingers tightened around the back of her skull.

Maybe he's serious, she thought. *Maybe he's really going to twist until my neck snaps.*

The rabbit's ears stood up. He put more force into his arm, and her neck twisted to an almost impossible degree. Her muscles cried out in unimaginable pain. Yukiko grunted as saliva started to run out from the edges of her lips.

I'm... I'm going to die.

As her head turned past ninety degrees, her mind struggled to find any avenue for survival.

Still twisting her head, the rabbit leaned its weight against her and threw her to the floor. First she felt the sting of the concrete, and then the rabbit's fur enveloped her.

"I have to do this," he said. "I just want you to know that. There's no other way."

The rabbit bent his arm, and her neck craned with it. She could no longer breathe. Convulsions shot through her body. She began to lose her vision, as if a strip of gauze had been placed over her eyes.

Is this what it's like to die?

In her mind's eye, she saw herself as a little girl. She was giggling, cradling a dirty doll in her arms.

So it's true then, what they say—that the moment you die, your life flashes before your eyes. Is this the moment I die? I don't want to die!

Her refusal to let go of life roused her from her descent into death.

I can't die here. I can't die at the hands of this rabbit.

Her eyes opened wide.

Yukiko could see the side of the water tower just beyond the rabbit's furry arm. Valves of various sizes came out from the side of the tower. Below them was a row of metal outflow spigots.

Yukiko reached for a red valve and turned it. The valve hadn't been worked loose in a long time, and Yukiko was not particularly strong to begin with. She shouldn't have been able to turn it, but her determination to survive gave her the strength she needed.

With a deafening roar, reddish-brown water sprayed from the spigot. The torrent hit the rabbit perfectly in the face and knocked him backward. Yukiko rolled to the side, got to her feet, and scrambled to the opposite side of the water tower, while the gushing water pushed the rabbit almost all the way back to the top of the stairs.

Yukiko peeked around the far side of the tank and saw the rabbit reeling in pain and confusion. She nodded with satisfaction.

She had her opening, but now she needed to do something with it. She focused with every scrap of willpower she possessed.

Her eyes glistened.

She had an idea.

The rabbit was soaked through, every last hair matted to his body. Coughing and sputtering, he slowly stood. The pain from the torrential water's impact was matched by the anguish at being taken so completely by surprise.

The rabbit despaired.

While he had been struggling against the seemingly endless deluge, Yukiko had almost certainly escaped. By now, she probably wasn't even in the department store. How would he ever be able to catch her again?

His ears drooped, and he sank down onto the concrete floor.

He had been so close. Just a few moments longer, and he'd have taken his beloved Yukiko's life with his own hands. A few moments longer, and he'd have twisted her head fully backward, and she would have been dead.

He looked up to the sky through eyelids half closed over by blood.

Scaffolding had been erected around and above the water tank that had brought about his failure. It looked like the building's owners were intending on installing an even larger reservoir. The scaffolding held platforms that spiraled up to the top of the tank, with more framework going higher still, leaving a void in the middle.

Slowly, he put a hand on one of the scaffolding tubes and leaned back against the wall next to the stairway door. For now, he needed a break. He'd get some energy back, gather himself, and think of how he would handle Yukiko.

His ears folded back against his head, and his eyes closed — but then he let loose a small, startled exclamation and opened his eyes. He sensed someone nearby. Above. Someone was above him.

His ears stood straight up as he looked up at the scaffolding. "She's... she's here." Yukiko was there.

He had been wrong. She hadn't escaped far away, but was right there, partway up the scaffolding.

Yukiko was standing still, gripping the guardrail, but when the rabbit took his first awkward, water-soaked step onto the decking, she quickly turned and began ascending the ramp to the next platform.

"Yukiko," the rabbit rumbled, "give it up. You've got nowhere to run."

With her lithe body, Yukiko climbed her way from

level to level with ease, while the rabbit's encumbered, leaden steps prevented him from closing in. In the end, that wouldn't matter, because what the rabbit said was right. Once she'd reached the top of the structure, there was nowhere farther for her to go. Even if he couldn't catch up with her before then, he would still reach her.

Yukiko must have known that, but still she climbed.

There was no guarantee she'd even manage to ascend that far. The scaffolding was by no means sturdy. With each step she took, the platforms shook, and the connecting bolts gave a loud and dissonant creak. Even attempting the ascent was dangerous—and that was only under her comparatively light weight. The giant, water-logged rabbit was climbing after her now, and he was much heavier.

When Yukiko neared the top of the water tower, she stumbled and leaned against the guardrail. The platform had suddenly bowed beneath her. It seemed that some careless worker had only half-fastened the bolts in that section.

Yukiko looked down, and her head spun. The water tower stood several stories tall above the rest of the roof. She had a fear of heights, though not on the same level as James Stewart in Hitchcock's *Vertigo*. Still, she clung to the handrail and did her best not to look down again.

Yet she couldn't just remain standing there, without

doing anything. The rabbit, slow as he was, was coming for her, closing in. She risked another glance down and found that he was quite close now, moving faster even as his footsteps made the rickety scaffolding creak and groan.

Yukiko looked up. At the top of the tower was a small square landing just one meter long on each side. The terminus of the water tower. The only way back down was the same way the rabbit was coming up.

She could hear him now, muttering in that scratchy voice. "Yu…ki…ko."

The rabbit's fingertips appeared on the lip of the platform one level down. Yukiko drew in her legs and hugged her arms around her knees. The rabbit laughed and ran the remaining distance with surprising speed. And then his hand was on her ankle. His grip was incredibly strong. She kicked her leg as hard as she could, but his fingers held on tight.

Slowly, he pulled her toward him by the ankle. As her body was dragged down, the rabbit rose up and soon their faces met. The rabbit let out a delighted sigh.

As she suffered under the stench of his rotten-meat body odor, she moved a hand behind her back and begin loosening one of the bolts holding the scaffolding together. When it had been first constructed, the bolt would have been far too tight to loosen with her bare hands, but after extended exposure to wind and small vibrations, the bolt had gradually worked itself loose.

Careful not to let the rabbit catch on, she shifted her weight toward the wall of the tower so that the scaffolding pressed against the tower's surface. With some of the strain taken off the bolt, it began to turn more easily. The bolt had rusted over, and Yukiko still had trouble turning it, but as she kept putting her muscle into it, the layer of rust flaked away, and the bolt itself popped free from the joint.

Yukiko shoved at the rabbit's face with both hands and threw her weight backward. With a shrill creak, the scaffolding sagged and began tipping away from the tank.

Taken by surprise, the rabbit let go of Yukiko and grabbed for the scaffold's vertical tube—which was quickly becoming rather less vertical. Yukiko hooked her arm around the railing at the top landing, lifted her feet, and used her stomach muscles to raise her lower body up and onto the platform.

The scaffolding began to buckle under the rabbit's weight, and it twisted toward the next section where the bolt still held. The rabbit's platform traced a wide and slow arc until it came back to slam into the side of the tower.

The rabbit's hand jolted free from the handhold, and he smacked hard into the wall. Pancaked against the curved surface, he slid and skidded down, gravity winning the fight against friction. As he fell, his arms searched about for anything to grab that might arrest his descent, but they found nothing.

Yukiko sat motionless on the platform atop the water tower.

She was relieved to have defeated the rabbit, but now it seemed she was stuck, with nothing to do but wait until help came for her.

Since panicking would get her nowhere, she simply sat hugging her knees while gazing up at the empty sky.

After watching the rabbit fall with the scaffolding, she was confident he couldn't have survived. Though she felt a little uneasy being entirely alone on her high-up perch, she was free from the terror the rabbit had struck into her.

What she didn't know was that the rabbit, driven by his obsession, was slowly working his way back up the tower. He took whatever small handholds it had to offer, moving his oversized body with the deftness of a rock climber.

Holding fast to the curved wall, he climbed all the way to the top. When he crested the top edge, he saw Yukiko on the platform, her back turned to him. A low laugh of victory threatened to come up, but he stifled it so as not to spoil the surprise.

The metal railing of the upper platform was nearly within his grasp.

When they had at long last managed to quell the mass panic, Kanda and Yoriko went to the roof to look for Yukiko.

"Where in the world could she have gone?" Yoriko wondered.

Kanda said, "If she wasn't in the green room or backstage, she must be out on the roof somewhere. She probably waited for everything to settle down and then went out there to find us."

From the stage, they looked out across the vacant roof. The scattered heaps of folding chairs spoke to the severity of the chaos that had occurred.

"Surely she wouldn't have left the department store," Kanda said, sounding unsure. "Would she?"

"Not a chance," Yoriko replied. She surveyed the rooftop with worry in her eyes. "She may be young, but she has a strong sense of duty. She wouldn't have left her fans—or us—behind."

"You're right. Well, where else could she be?" Kanda thought for a while, then muttered, "Wait, what about…" Then to Yoriko, he said, "Follow me," and started jogging to the emergency stairs. "The original part of the building has its own little roof—it's still there today. Maybe that's where she went!"

Yoriko hurried after him.

The rusty door opened onto a small, dilapidated roof dominated by a weatherworn water tower.

Yoriko shouted, "Up there!"

Kanda saw it at the same time.

Yukiko was sitting, arms around her knees, at the top of the half-collapsed scaffolding. She seemed to be staring off into the distance, lost in her thoughts—oblivious to the monster coming up on her from behind, his arms spread wide.

Opening his mouth so wide his jaw might have fallen off, Kanda shouted, "Yukiko! Behind you! Yukiko!"

But even yelling as loud as he could, his voice didn't reach her.

The rabbit put his hands on her shoulders. Watching helplessly from below, Yoriko could feel his fingers digging painfully into her flesh, as if she were the one up there.

Yukiko remained still, stoically enduring the rabbit's cruel touch.

"That's good," Yoriko said. "Don't upset him. Fighting will only make things worse. Just do as he says." If Yukiko tried to fight him off and failed, it might anger him into doing something terrible.

Yukiko couldn't have heard her, but she seemed to have gotten the message, as she remained entirely pliant and passive. Whether she was choosing not to struggle or just didn't have the strength left to try it, Yoriko didn't know. Whatever the case, complying with the rabbit was the safest route.

"Yoriko-kun, bring the police," Kanda said. "And get word to management and security."

He put his hand on what remained of the scaffolding and began attempting the ascent. Before he could start, Yoriko let out an unearthly scream that was so loud her heart might have leapt out from her throat.

Kanda froze.

He looked up with eyes open wide. The rabbit had grabbed Yukiko's head and was twisting it as if she were a doll. By the time he looked up, the rabbit had already wrenched her head around more than ninety degrees.

The rabbit's shoulders rose as he put even more force into his hands, turning Yukiko's head fully backward.

Kanda's face went pale.

Unable to bear the sight of such madness and cruelty, Yoriko covered her face with both hands and slumped to the concrete.

The rabbit kept on turning her head right and left and right again until it popped clear off. He swung her head against the water tower over and over and over, cackling as he did so. Then he tossed Yukiko's head up into the sky. It traced a tall arc until it gradually gave way to gravity, slowing down and beginning its descent.

The head crashed into the concrete roof exactly halfway between Kanda and Yoriko. It landed with a heavy *thunk* and crumbled into course powder.

Yoriko stared at the dust in blinking disbelief. She leaned over what had become of Yukiko's head.

"This," she said, "is this...plaster?"

Yukiko, dressed only in her underwear, came running out from the other side of the water tower.

Kanda and Yoriko cried her name in unison, but she held up a palm to quiet them. She beckoned the two over and handed them a rope that hung down from the platform atop the tower. Speaking only through looks and gestures, she signaled for them to pull the rope as hard as they could.

Kanda nodded in understanding, and Yoriko tightened her grip on the rope, whispering, "That was the replica, wasn't it?"

Yukiko nodded.

Above them, the rabbit screeched, "Yu...ki...ko!"

As if that were their cue, the three put all their combined strength into pulling the rope. They pulled it with all their focus and all their weight.

The supports beneath the platform hadn't been

sturdy in the first place, and they collapsed as readily as if they were made of taffy. The platform began to tilt, and the rabbit rolled forward.

Yukiko's replica was the first to slide off, and the rabbit came tumbling down immediately after, as if still in pursuit. As they both fell, the rabbit caught the life-size doll in his arms and drew it into a deep embrace.

Speed increasing, he slammed against a water valve jutting from the side of the tower. He rebounded out and over the rooftop's guardrail and then down toward the street below in an unwitting dive toward his death.

Yukiko patted Yoriko on the back with a rope-burned hand. Yoriko embraced her, covering the singer's un-clothed body.

"It's over," Yoriko said. "It's over, Yukiko-chan."

In her arms, Yukiko nodded several times.

Yoriko took off her jacket and gave it to Yukiko, then walked to the rooftop's guardrail and leaned out to look down below.

Yukiko's life-size twin figure had fragmented against the pavement directly in front of the department store's entrance. Several hundred curious onlookers were gathering around the doll's remains.

But somehow, inexplicably, the rabbit suit was gone.

"I can't believe it," Yoriko said. "What could have happened? He was dead. He had to be."

Yoriko and Yukiko's eyes met.

As if to herself, Yukiko said, "What was he?"

Kanda looked off into the clouds floating far in the distance. Softly, he said, "Maybe he was a phantom. Maybe that's what he was all along—a monster conjured by jealousy and obsession."

Yukiko simply nodded.

PERFECT
BLUE

AFTERWORD

◇

To tell the truth, the opening story, "Wake Me from This Dream," is something of a test piece I wrote while I was still a novice fiction writer. After starting my career in publishing (as a publishing producer), I became a columnist at age twenty-nine. As I recall, this story was written when I was around thirty.

When I reread the story now, what I find most deeply interesting is how the inextricable relationship between pop idol and stalker established itself as a central theme in my works from the very start. My second story, "Cry Your Tears," and my third (and first full-length novel), *Perfect Blue: Complete Metamorphosis*, both shared the theme. My fourth story, "Even When I Embrace You," did too. My fifth, *Simple Red*, didn't have an idol for the protagonist. Instead, the novel followed a woman who was an anime voice actor. But, like idols, voice actors are also afflicted by stalkers among their fans.

Why am I so fascinated by the conflict between idol and stalker? One reason that comes to mind is my belief that the very concept of an idol includes an element of stalking in its makeup.

Let me explain what I mean. Everyone, man and woman alike, has some degree of a stalker somewhere in their nature. I suggest that idols act as a catalyst that radically heightens and intensifies that common trait. The existence or absence of this perhaps detrimental power is directly connected to whether or not that person is truly an idol. No matter how some advertisers might promote a new talent as "a twenty-first century idol," if that idol doesn't have the associated power, then they're not an idol. Conversely, if someone not generally considered to be an idol—for example, an assistant on a cooking show, or a local TV newscaster—does possess that power, then they're as much an idol as anyone.

I didn't write "Wake Me from This Dream" with the intention of publishing it as a professional writer. At the time, I was with a couple friends when one said, "We should try to write something as a competition." Being interested in writing as a profession, I immediately agreed. I finished the piece and handed it over before the deadline. That in itself gave me a sense of accomplishment, but even still, I only had two readers. I remember feeling vaguely unfulfilled. But now that story has been published in this book—and the cover of that book (the Japanese edition) is graced by an original painting by the world-renowned artist, Martiros Manoukian. On top of that, the story is being made into a live-action movie coming to theaters this summer (2002). What a world of difference that is from only being read by two people.

"Wake Me from This Dream" was the starting point of my career as a writer, and as its creator, I feel deeply and genuinely happy to be able to watch it grow.

—Yoshikazu Takeuchi

PERFECT BLUE